BOOMERANG SPACESHIP

Trent, captain of the space freighter *Yarrow*, came of a long line of spaceship commanders ... and all of them had been troubled by pirates. Due to the nature of the space drive, which permitted flight to the stars past the speed of light, ships in flight were in more danger to each other than from anything else. It was this ability of one ship's drive to blow out any drive near it that made space pirates so difficult to eradicate.

But this time Trent went into overdrive with a special device aboard—one that would turn the tables and make space permanently barred to pirates.

Trent was skeptical himself—and his skepticism stood him in good stead when he found himself more pirate bait than pirate baiter—and his secret weapon a space-warping double-edged boomerang.

MURRAY LEINSTER

novels available in Ace editions:

SPACE CAPTAIN

by

MURRAY LEINSTER

ACE BOOKS, INC.
1120 Avenue of the Americas
New York, N.Y. 10036

I

H E CAME OF a long line of ship captains, which probably explains the whole matter. His grandfather was the Captain Trent who found the hole in the Coalsack, that monstrous dust cloud between Syrtis and the whole Galliene region, and thereby cut months from the time formerly needed to go around the Coalsack to the new colonies beyond it. A great-great-great-grandfather was the Captain Trent who charted the interstellar meteoric streams in the Enid group of suns, whereby no less than eight highly desirable planets became available for human occupation, and one was named after him.

Farther back still, a many-more-times-great-grandfather commanded the second colony-ship to reach Delva. He arrived to find the first arrivals hysterical with terror and demanding to be taken off and carried home, which couldn't be done with his ship already loaded to capacity. But that Captain Trent went into the jungles with eight spacemen and found out the activity cycle of the giant saurians who'd ap-

peared to make the colony impossible. Now there was a gam
refuge for those beasts, carefully watched lest an interesting
species be wiped out by hide-hunters.

There were other Captain Trents, all the way back to
who skippered a trading ship in the eighteenth century, wh
ships sailed oceans of water only, and a coasting-voyage
from London to Scotland took as long a time as nowadays
from Rigel to Punt, and when a sailing ship took as long to
reach the Azores as is now required for the sixty-light-
year journey from Deneb to Kildare.

But the similarity between such sailing and modern jour-
neying did not end with the time between ports. In those
early days, as now, a ship leaving harbor was strictly on its
own until it dropped anchor again. There was, as today, no
communication between ports except by ship. Hence a cargo
in strong demand in a given port last week might be worth-
less in an overstocked market this week, because in the interval one ship or two had come in with the same commodity
to offer. So in those days, as now, all ship captains were
traders. They bought wisely and sold shrewdly, depending
on a percentage of the voyage's profits for their reward.

Also, then as now, there were ships which left port and
were never heard of more. Some struck reefs and some per-
ished in storms. But other dangers were of human origin,
and that Captain Trent of the eighteenth century was not
gentle with their originators.

It was related of him that he once sailed into an English
port with shot-holes in his sails and patches on his hull and
a fished repair to his foremast, and with hanged men swing-
ing at his yardarms. He explained curtly that a pirate had
attacked his ship and he couldn't spare hands to guard those
who surrendered, so he'd hanged them. At the time he was
much admired. But he was forgotten now. Yet a great-great-
great-and-so-on-grandson of that Captain Trent was the
captain of the space-merchantman *Yarrow*, who made the
most profitable voyage of any ship captain so far recorded.

It didn't look promising at its outset. The *Yarrow* was an
elderly merchant ship of a size becoming unprofitable in

modern times. Her record, though, was honorable. She was driven by old and dependable Lawlor engines which faithfully thrust her through emptiness at a good speed in normal space, but a good many times faster than light when an overdrive field surrounded her hull. There had never been any trouble with her air, and she'd been surveyed in her fortieth year and certified for voyages of any length in the galaxy. But her size was against her. A skipper who could make money with her would be better employed in a larger ship. It would require very special conditions to make it profitable to send her to space again.

But those conditions did exist. The owners of the *Yarrow* explained them to Captain Trent. He listened. They mentioned that space commerce in the Pleiad group was almost at an end. It was bad enough that a privateer had been commissioned by the government of Loren to force trade with that unprosperous planet. That was very bad—legal, perhaps, but undesirable. But out-and-out piracy had been practiced to such a degree that even the pirates of the Pleiads now complained of the poor state of business. Hence the possibility of good profits and the offer of the ship to Captain Trent.

The owners of the *Yarrow* explained that magnificent profits could be earned even by a ship of the *Yarrow*'s size in a trading voyage to the Pleiads if, first, she had a skipper of Captain Trent's ability to handle her, and, second, if she was equipped with a defense against pirates that had been developed by one of the space-line's ship engineers.

Trent observed that he didn't hold with gadgets. He seemed reluctant. The owners raised their offer. Fifteen percent of the voyage's profits instead of ten to the skipper. An absolutely free hand in the choice of ports to be called at. His own selection of cargo to be put on board. His own crew. A guarantee of so much for making the voyage, whether profitable or not.

These were very unusual concessions. Captain Trent listened, apparently unconvinced. The owners sweated. They explained urgently that the *Yarrow* was a dead loss while it

remained idle. They were anxious to get it out to space.
They added as a final lure that they would send McHinny
along to be the ship's engineer and operate the pirate-
frustrating device. He was its inventor. He'd be the ideal
operator. The *Yarrow* would be safe against danger from
pirates, which had practically stopped trade between the
solar systems of the Pleiads. What more did he want? Salvage rights? He could have them too.

It was a custom of owners to offer salvage rights when they
wanted to convince a skipper of their generosity. Salvage
rights amounted to an agreement that if Captain Trent should
find an opportunity for salvage, in space or aground, that he
could make use of the *Yarrow* for the job, provided only that
he paid charter-rate for the use of the ship during salvage
operations.

Captain Trent smiled politely and, after reflection, accepted the proposal. The *Yarrow*'s owners clapped him on
the back and congratulated him on their generosity, and then
feverishly got the *Yarrow* ready to lift off. In three days the
ship was loaded with cargo Trent had approved. The landing-grid lifted her to space. And then the owners relaxed,
gratefully.

Because this was the day before the insurance rates on
ships and cargos for the Pleiads were to be raised to twenty-
four percent. The *Yarrow*'s owners had wanted to get her
off ground before that rise in premiums. As Trent saw it, if
he did make the voyage and get home again, there'd be a
good profit for the owners. But if he didn't return, they'd
collect full-value insurance on the *Yarrow* and her cargo.
Trent was aware that on the whole they'd prefer the insurance.

It didn't bother him. Prices should be high and profits
excellent in a sector of space where space commerce had become so hazardous that pirates themselves had run up against
the law of diminishing returns.

Trent checked the *Yarrow*'s position by sighting and iden-
tifying the planet Gram. But he didn't go aground there.

He went back into overdrive and drove around the Beta Cloud—an isolated space-danger a light-year in extent, the result of a semi-nova outbreak of the sun in its middle—and made his first landing at Dorade. He learned that the situation of piracy and grounding of space craft still existed in the Pleiads. Here, thriftily, he made two deals. One was for the sale of some not particularly desirable cargo, and the other was the purchase of small arms and police equipment manufactured for export to other planets' police departments. It amounted to a swap of this for that. He learned that the state of things in the Pleiads was worse. Most skippers stayed out of the Pleiads altogether. Interstellar trade in general had been cut by ninety per cent among the Pleiad worlds. Some shipowners there had sent their ships far away, with instructions not to return while space travel was so perilous in their home stellar group. Some had grounded all their ships. The only real communication between inhabited planets of the Pleiads was by small space craft not worth a pirate's or a privateer's attention. But there weren't many of them.

Trent judged this to be a promising state of things. He lifted off from Dorade. On the next leg of his journey he instructed his crewmen in the use of the just-acquired weapons. In particular he drilled them in the fine art of combat inside a spaceship's elquences of compartments, tanks, holds, and other places they'd never imagined as combat areas. They found the instructions fascinating. He informed them of practical but unusual methods by which men in spaceboats could board other space craft, using shaped charges against a metal hull to give them entry. These instructions, of course, were to prepare against pirates.

The *Yarrow*'s crewmen were charmed. They formed a zestful conviction that Captain Trent planned some highly profitable piracy himself. They learned their novel lessons with enthusiasm and hope.

The *Yarrow* went on its way. Trent's several-times-great grandfather would have kept his crew chipping paint or tightening or slacking off stays to adjust to differences of humidity from day to day. If they were merchant seamen, they already knew how to fight. But Trent exercised his crew with weapons.

They anticipated interesting consequences of their new combat efficiency. They looked at Trent with bright eyes, waiting for him to tell them they were about to capture a space liner loaded with treasure and with terrified and hence docile females.

He gave them no such information, but he did keep them busy. Presently the *Yarrow* landed on Midway. He went aground, alone. He asked questions. He admitted that he planned to go trading in the Pleiads.

Officials on Midway warned him solicitously. Only one ship had left Midway for the Pleiads in months. None at all had come from them. The one ship to risk going in was the *Hecla,* and she'd lifted off only the day before. Her skipper'd judged from the latest reports of missing ships that the pirates were working on the far side of the Pleiad group. He was making a full-power dash for Loren. Trent had better not imitate him.

But Trent did. He lifted the *Yarrow* off Midway after only three hours aground. Immediately she was in space again he had the small-arms weapons passed out once more.

For four days out of Midway the *Yarrow* drove steadily, in overdrive and of course in illimitable isolation. She was surrounded by her overdrive field. Through it no light could pass, nor any message of any kind but one. Every instrument aboard her, made to report on the universe outside, now read zero. It was as if there were no cosmos, no galaxy, no existence beyond the ship's hull plates. The viewports viewed nothing. The communicators received nothing. The *Yarrow* was isolated as earlier generations could not have imagined. In overdrive a ship is practically in another and an empty universe, in which nothing ever happens.

But on the fourth shipday out from Midway one solitary instrument gave a reading. One dial-needle stirred, in the control room. One detector-needle moved the minutest possible trivial indication. A light glowed. The spaceman on control room watch notified Trent through the loudspeaker in the captain's cabin.

"Captain, sir, the drive-detector's registering."

"I'll be there immediately," said Trent.

He was. It was less than five yards from his cabin to the control room, but he hurried. The broad instrument board faced him as he entered, with all its dials and indicators above the equally broad but less cluttered lower control panel. Underneath every instrument either a green or an amber light told that each unit of the ship's equipment either operated normally, or was ready to do so when the ship broke out of overdrive. But the light under the overdrive detector shone red.

"No change as yet, sir," said the man on watch.

Trent grunted. He sat down in the pilot's chair. Almost immediately he reversed the *Yarrow's* drive. It began to cut down her speed from unthinkable overdrive-velocity to thousands of miles a minute, then to hundreds, to tens.

The detector reported stronger and stronger indications of another over-drive operating within another ship a—now—relatively trivial number of miles away. It would have to be in a ship, of course. And that ship would be informed by a detector in its control room of the *Yarrow's* existence and near presence.

Trent threw a switch. A panel of signal-analyzing instruments lit up. He set to work with them.

There was silence save for that small assortment of noises any ship makes while it is driving. It means that the ship is going somewhere, and hence that it will eventually arrive somewhere. A ship in port with all operating devices cut off seems gruesomely dead. Few spacemen will stay aboard ship in a spaceport. The silence is too oppressive.

The signal-analyzer clicked. It had determined the bearing of the other overdrive field. Lighted numerals preserved the information while the analyzers investigated other items. The detected field was very faint. Its bearing was ten-forty to the *Yarrow's* course. Its own course—

It had no course. If one allowed for the *Yarrow*'s motion, the other ship must be standing still. But this was light-years away from Midway, and Midway was still the nearest world. It was not normal for a ship to lie still in space between the stars. Trent did something more abnormal still. He headed the *Yarrow* toward the overdrive signal source.

He pushed the all-hands-alert button. Speakers all over the ship emitted the raucous warning of probable emergency. He spoke into a microphone, and the same speakers echoed his words with a peculiar choral effect.

"Load small arms," he ordered curtly. "Take combat posts. Rocket launchers to the airlocks. No launching without orders."

He settled more firmly in the pilot's chair, and the man on watch drew back and began to get out the spacesuits the control-room occupants might need next. Trent continued to watch the dials of the signal-analysis devices. He had only instrument readings to go by now, but in all other respects this development in the journey of the *Yarrow* was like the sighting of a sail when one of his ancestors captained a trading vessel in the eighteenth century. The report of a reading on the drive detector was equivalent to a bellowed *"Sail ho!"* from a sailing brig's crosstrees. Trent's painstaking use of signal-analysis instruments was equal to his ancestor's going aloft to use his telescope on a minute speck at the horizon. What might follow could continue to duplicate in utterly changed conditions what had happened in simpler times, in sailing ship days.

The *Yarrow*'s mate came in.

"Spacesuits, sir?" he asked stolidly.

"Better put them on, yes," agreed Trent. He didn't take his eyes from the instruments. The mate gave the order. He put on a spacesuit himself, from the back wall of the control room.

"Any other orders, sir?"

"Eh? Yes. Make sure the engineer's gadget is set for operation. We might as well try it out. But the engineer's the kind of putterer who'll constantly be trying to improve it. If he's done anything, make him stop and get it ready for use."

"Yes, sir," said the mate.

"You'd better know what's going on," added Trent. "There's an overdrive field out there ahead. It's of detection strength only; it isn't strong enough to affect the ship that's emitting it. But it should mean that our drive has been picked up too. Yet we're headed for it and it hasn't moved. You figure that out!"

Ships in overdrive avoid each other carefully, for self-evident reasons. But the *Yarrow* was driving toward a ship which was not in motion but should have known of the *Yarrow*'s approach. It had a very weak field in existence, so weak that it couldn't possibly do anything but notify the *Yarrow*'s presence and approach. But it hadn't moved!

The mate blinked and struggled with the problem.

"Maybe we'd better keep away, sir," he suggested.

Trent finished sealing his own spacesuit. He put on the helmet and opened the face plate.

"Go see that the engineer's gadget is ready for use," he commanded. "I'll try it first."

The mate went out. Trent shrugged his shoulders. No ship in pirate-infested space should lie still, emitting a weak drive field which was an invitation to pirates to approach. The fact that one did exactly that suggested a very specific event in the course of happening. The mate didn't see it, which was possibly why he was still a mate.

The *Yarrow* continued to approach the source of a feeble overdrive field, capable at this strength only of operating as a detector of other overdrive fields. But the *Yarrow*'s approach didn't cause it to move, either to avoid the *Yarrow* or to attack it. Which was also unreasonable. It suggested that the crewmen of the other ship had some enterprise in hand which was too absorbing to let anybody bother about instruments.

Trent's expression was at once formidable and absorbed. The formidable part was much the stronger. His lips were a firm straight line. From his pilot's chair he surveyed the control board again. The signal-analysis setup continued to work, re-observing the data which was all it could report.

The source of the remarkably weak detector field was a thousand miles away. Five hundred. Two hundred. One. Trent said in a clipped voice, "Engine room! Is that gadget ready for use?"

The mate's voice replied from a speaker.

"Just a minute, sir. The engineer says he was improving it. But he's getting it back together, sir."

Trent swore, in a level voice. He swung the *Yarrow* a second time in the infinite blackness of overdrive. The other ship would be in normal space. It's drive was turned to detector-strength only, which meant that it couldn't do anything but detect other drives. That other ship would see the Milky Way and a thousand million stars. The *Yarrow*, approaching it, saw nothing. It was like one of those legendary submarines of the wars on Earth. It was blind and invisible because it was in overdrive, but it came nearer and nearer to its unseen quarry.

Trent said shortly, "All hands close face plates. Use air from your suit tanks. I'm breaking out of overdrive. Engine room, how about that gadget?"

The mate's voice, troubled, "Another minute, sir! Not more than another minute!"

Trent said in the iciest of voices, "I'm breaking out now. Let me know when to start charging it. Rocket launchers, stay ready but wait for orders."

Then he turned the overdrive switch to "OFF."

He felt, of course, those acutely unpleasant sensations which always accompany entering or leaving the overdrive state. One is acutely dizzy and horribly nauseated for the fraction of a second. One has the helpless feeling of falling through a contracting spiral. Then, suddenly, it is all over.

The *Yarrow* was back in normal space.

But the nearest-object dial registered something impossibly close. The dead-ahead screen showed what Trent had guessed at. It showed the other ship and why it was still. It even showed why nobody was paying attention to the readings of drive-detector instruments.

Twenty miles away from where the *Yarrow* had just broken out of overdrive, a bulky merchantman lay dead in space. Two miles from it a smaller, lighter ship stood by. Spaceboats from the smaller vessel were pulling toward the larger ship.

The situation was self-explanatory. A pirate or a privateer had blown the overdrive of a merchantman, most probably the *Hecla* out of Midway and bound for the Pleiads, for Loren. The merchantman had evidently been crippled so it could not flee. And as it lay helpless, boats from the pirate ship were now moving to board their victim. And the crewmen of the marauder were too busy watching to notice detector dials.

II

THE EMERGENCE OF the *Yarrow* from overdrive would naturally set strident gongs to ringing in both the other ships. The space-communicator speaker in the ceiling of the control room babbled frantically, *"Mayday! Mayday! Calling for help! A pirate has blown our overdrive and shelled us! Mayday! Mayday! Hel—"*

There was a crashing noise in the speaker. The wail for aid from the merchantman was blotted out and destroyed by a monstrous pure white noise. It came from the smaller ship. Somebody in the control room there had been stung to action by the *Yarrow's* breakout. He'd seen, at last, the visible detector signal, and as a first emergency reaction he'd turned loose pure noise. It jammed the rest of the distress call and would have made coöperation between the *Yarrow* and the *Hecla* impossible, had it been possible in the first place.

The speaker made other noises, originating in the engine room. Trent swore. He flipped off the communicator from the need to have in-ships reports. The mate's voice came, startlingly clear:

"Gadget's ready to charge, sir. The engineer says so. You can charge the gadget."

Ahead where the two strange craft lay, the spaceboats from the smaller one reversed their motion and raced back toward the ship from which they'd come. That vessel continued to transmit a powerful blast of ear-splitting sound, the reception of which Trent had just stopped. The merchantman continued to beg frantically for help.

"Go ahead, sir," repeated the mate from the *Yarrow's* engine room. *"It's all right to charge."*

Trent fumbled for the first of the two new controls on the instrument board. The first should draw on the drive circuit for thousands of kilowatts to charge the gadget's power bank of capacitors. It should continue to draw for minutes. Then a tripping of the second new control should mean the discharge of energy in one blast of power that ought to blow the pirate's drive and leave it helpless and limited to normal-space drive.

This could be done only with both ships in overdrive. But Trent was confident that he could force the pirate into that quasi-cosmos and there let the gadget cripple it, forcing it back to normality where it might be dealt with. He had only police-type rockets, to be sure, but there were other means. In any case, at the least and worst he should be able to take off the *Hecla's* ship's company and carry them to port, and then return with better weapons to finish off the pirate. He should be able to do it before it could rewind its overdrive.

His fingers found the charging switch. Thrown, it should begin to charge up. In minutes it would be ready. The pirate could be gotten into overdrive where it would expect to blow the *Yarrow's* drive. But its own field generator should flash and arc and perhaps even melt down.

He threw the charging switch.

There was a racking, crashing explosion in the engine

room. The smell of vaporized metal and burnt insulation spread through the *Yarrow*. There were shoutings.

The mate came into the control room. His spacesuit showed signs of having been spattered with exploded bits of wire insulator.

"That gadget," he said with unbelievable stolidity, "it blew out. It didn't work. It blew when you turned it on."

Trent was too much enraged even to swear. He'd tried the gadget the *Yarrow*'s owners swore by and touted. He'd thrown away the advantage of surprise. Now he was only miles away from an undoubtedly armed pirate which was acutely aware of his presence.

It would have been logical for him to tear his hair in total frustration, and such a reaction would have seemed as useful as any other. But he stared at the spaceboats streaking back toward the pirate ship. It would take them so long to get back and so much longer to get into the spaceboat blisters in which they were carried. The pirate could blow the *Yarrow*'s drive if she went into overdrive. The *Yarrow* couldn't blow the pirate's. Trent could only put up a fight in normal space with the odds on the pirate. The only fact in his favor was that the pirate wouldn't follow him into overdrive until it had its spaceboats back aboard. It was possible for him to maneuver in a fashion peculiarly like a submarine —one of those fabulous weapons of the last wars on Earth —submerging to get out of sight, but only until the pirate's spaceboats were stowed again.

He used that antiquated maneuver. The *Yarrow* vanished, only to reappear seconds later in normal space once more and very much nearer to the pirate.

The spaceboats were nearly back home, then. The pirate swung, and there was one of those extraordinarily hurried bursts of smoke which appear when an explosive is set off in emptiness. Vapor appeared and fled madly to nothingness. A shell went hurtling madly to nowhere. The pirate had a gun. The *Hecla* had said it had been shelled. Trent took the *Yarrow* into overdrive again. The symptoms of nausea and dizziness and crazy spiral fall were multiplied in their unpleasantness by being repeated after so short an interval.

The time lapse before its return to normal space was very short. It was only seconds, but the spaceboats were alongside the pirate and the mussel-shell-shaped covers of the lifeboat blisters were already opening to receive them. But the *Yarrow* was only hundreds of yards away, now, and Trent flung it into full-speed-ahead emergency drive.

The *Yarrow* rushed upon the pirate ship like something infuriated and deadly. It was the most improbable of all possible maneuvers. There were stars on every hand, and above and below to boot. There was no solidity for distances no human being had yet been able to comprehend. With all of space in which to maneuver or attempt to flee, with an enemy come from beyond the nearer stars, Trent was attempting the absolutely earliest and most primitive of naval combat tactics. Ramming. And it was partly successful.

The pirate ship let off a panicky shell at the *Yarrow*. It missed. Before the gun could be fired again the *Yarrow* was upon it. Steel hull plates crumpled and tore. The bigger ship plunged into the lesser one, with all its interior ringing from the screech of rent metal.

And the pirate vanished. It had gone into overdrive at the last and ultimate instant, while its bow plates were actually crumpling. The *Yarrow* plunged through the emptiness the pirate left behind. It turned and plunged again, and again, and yet again, like something huge and enraged trying to trample or to crush a small and agile foe.

There were only two ships left in normal space, here. One of course was the *Yarrow*. The other was the helpless merchantman *Hecla*. For the moment Trent ignored the other ship. He kept the *Yarrow* twisting and circling through the emptiness where the pirate had been. He kept the *Yarrow*'s own drive detector in operation, attempting to locate his enemy. He'd only damaged it in normal space, but if he followed it into overdrive—as things had worked out—it could cripple the *Yarrow* and then stand off and bombard it until no trace of life remained aboard. Had the men in the pirate's control room been alert, the pirate would have had adequate warning of the *Yarrow*'s coming.

But here and now the pirate ship stayed in overdrive and within detection-range for a considerable time. It might be evaluating the damage the *Yarrow*'s keel had done to it. But Trent listened icily, and heard the whine of its drive grow fainter and fainter until it died away. Then it must be either in normal space—but a very great distance off—or in overdrive and almost unimaginably distant.

It was an hour and more before Trent turned the *Yarrow* to the disabled *Hecla*. He'd turned off the spacephone speaker so he could listen to aboard-ship reports. Now he flipped it on again and a shaking, agitated voice came to him instantly.

"Please answer! Our hull is punctured by shells and we've had to put on our spacesuits because our air is going fast. A shell in the engine room knocked out our Lawlor drive and our overdrive coil is blown! Our situation is desperate! Please answer!"

Trent thumbed the transmitter button.

"Yarrow calling *Hecla,"* he said in a dry voice. "Under the circumstances, all I can do is take you aboard and get you to ground somewhere in safety. I can't linger around here. The pirate is damaged but apparently not destroyed. It went into overdrive when we hit it, and it's gotten away. Whether it can come back or not I don't know. Do you want to try to make repairs, gambling that it won't return?"

The voice from the *Hecla* was almost unintelligible in its frantic denial of any such idea and its haste to accept Trent's offer. Trent made brisk arrangements for the transfer of humans from the disabled ship. He shifted the *Yarrow* close alongside to make the transfer easier. He summoned the mate.

"You'll stay here," he commanded, "and you'll watch that detector! The pirate's men on watch were looking at the spaceboats so they didn't notice we were on the way. But you'll look at this and nothing else! And you'll report by spacephone if that needle even thinks of quivering!"

He made his way to the blister he'd emptied to receive

19

the *Hecla*'s boat and that helpless space craft's complement. In minutes he was aboard the *Hecla*. The air pressure was low. Very low. He went briskly over the wreck with the *Hecla*'s skipper, who would follow tradition and be the last man to abandon ship, but who was plainly not happy about delay.

"All right," said Trent, when he'd seen what damage the pirate's shelling had done. "Just one thing more. I want to look at the engine room again."

"If . . . if the pirate comes back—"

"It will be too bad," agreed Trent. "But just the same—"

He went into the *Hecla*'s engine room. The disabling of the *Hecla* had been very efficiently done. With the overdrive blown, the cargo boat was capable only of moving in unassisted Lawlor drive. It could make desperate darts and dashes here and there to postpone its inevitable doom. But that would be inconvenient for the pirate. It carried a gun for such occasions. It used it, and the *Hecla* could no longer have resisted.

At this moment the *Hecla*'s skipper was agitatedly pointing out that the pirate might come back.

Trent did not answer. He was busy in the engine room, reading dials, checking the fuse box. Having established a delay sequence he went with the *Hecla*'s now-quivering skipper to the airlock. The *Yarrow*'s bulk loomed up not forty feet away, but beneath and between the ships an unthinkable abyss lay. Stars shone up from between their feet. One could fall for millions of years and never cease to plummet through nothingness.

A *Yarrow* spaceman hauled them across and to the *Yarrow*'s open airlock at the ends of the space-rope lines. Instants later Trent was in the control room, his helmet off but otherwise attired for space. He stared out of the viewports. He began to frown, and then to scowl. The *Hecla*'s skipper came unsteadily to the control room door.

"I . . . I suggest," he said shakenly, "that we . . . get away from here as soon as possible."

"This is my ship," said Trent curtly. "I give the orders. Ah!"

He hadn't turned from the viewport. He'd been watching the *Hecla*, drained of air and without any living thing aboard, left as a derelict between the stars. But now the abandoned ship suddenly drew away from the *Yarrow*. She swung in space. She began to drive. She went away into the infinite distances between the suns of the galaxy. She dwindled to the tiniest of specks in the starlight. She disappeared altogether.

The *Hecla*'s skipper's mouth dropped open.

"What—"

"I don't like pirates," said Trent. "I'm afraid we didn't damage that one too badly, because it managed to stay in overdrive. But I didn't want it to come back and loot the *Hecla*. So I sent your ship driving off. Pure spite on my part."

"But what are we waiting for?" asked the skipper anxiously.

"Nothing now," Trent told him. "I've an errand in the engine room, but that can wait."

He examined the drive detector with almost microscopic care. It reported nothing. He set the *Yarrow* on course. He threw the drive switch. The *Yarrow* swept away from there.

Trent entered the engine room. It still smelled of vaporized metal and burnt insulator. McHinny paced up and down, swearing steadily and with undiminished indignation. He had invented the device which Trent had unsuccessfully used to blast the pirate ship. Now his gadget, which should have prevented all danger from the pirate ship, was a scorched, swollen, discolored wreck. A thread of smouldering insulation still sent a twig of gray smoke into the air above it.

"It didn't work," said Trent flatly. "What happened?"

McHinny was instantly and fiercely on the defensive. Hell hath no fury like an inventor defending his claim to genius.

"You didn't work it right!" he cried bitterly. "You ruined everything! You turned it on when there were two ships in range! Two! You overloaded it!"

Trent said nothing. This was defense, not fact. The *Hecla*'s drive had been burnt out by the pirate. It couldn't constitute half of an overload of overdrive tension.

"And the mate hurried me!" snapped McHinny furiously. "He kept saying I had to hurry and get it back together! I was improving it, and he rushed me to get it together again!"

Trent frowned. "Can you repair it?" he asked detachedly. "If it can be made to work we'll try it again."

"I'll have to rebuild it!" fumed the engineer. "And I won't stand for anybody telling me what to do! I invented it! I know all about it! I won't do anything unless I have a free hand!"

Trent raised his eyebrows. "All right," he said, "but we were lucky. Next time you remember that you're right in the same ship with the rest of us!"

He turned and started for the control room, contemplating his next move. The plans of the *Yarrow's* Captain Trent bore a strong family resemblance to the plan his ancestor had carried out in the days of sail. He believed that pirates did not like to fight. They preferred to murder. He suspected that they would be astonished if attacked, because they were accustomed only to attacking. And he believed that violent action when they didn't expect it might yield interesting results.

In short, his views were not those of the average trading-ship captain entering reluctantly into pirate-infested star groups. He'd had lively hopes of profitable action. He still might very well manage to find or contrive activity of a congenial kind. What he considered non-success in the *Hecla* matter only moved him to modify his intentions, not to abandon them.

There was a girl in the control room when he reëntered it. The *Hecla's* skipper spoke with something approaching reverence.

"Captain, Miss Hale wants to thank you. Her father is the planetary president of Loren."

Trent nodded politely. The girl said in a still unsteady voice, "I do want to thank you, Captain. If it hadn't been for you—"

22

"Only too pleased," said Trent as politely as before. "I'm glad we happened along."

"I . . . I can only offer words," said the girl, "but when we get to Loren, my father will at least—"

"I'm sorry, but I'm not going to Loren," said Trent. "The *Yarrow*'s bound for Sira. You'll go aground there."

The *Hecla*'s skipper said urgently, "But Captain Trent, this is Miss Hale! Her father's the planetary president. She was bound home. Surely you can swing ship off-course long enough to put her aground on her home world!"

Trent shook his head regretfully. A few hours earlier, he'd more or less intended to head for Loren himself. But events just past required a change of plan. The encounter with a pirate ship which had captured but not yet looted a merchantman hadn't ended the way he'd have wished. His plans had to be changed. They now called for an immediate call on Sira.

"I'm truly sorry," he said, "but I have to go to Sira. For one thing, it's three days nearer than Loren, and those three days are important to me."

"You don't realize—"

The girl put her hand on the skipper's arm. "No. If Captain Trent is bound for Sira, to Sira we go. I can surely get home from there! Of course we must get word to my father about the pirate pretending to be the *Bear*. But Captain Trent has surely done enough in saving us from . . . what would have happened if he hadn't appeared, and especially if he hadn't acted as he did."

Trent cocked his head inquiringly to one side.

"The *Bear?*"

"Our privateer," explained the girl. "We're on a terrible predicament on Loren. We have to have antibiotics, first, and what other off-planet supplies we can. But we have to have antibiotics! Our soil bacteria are death to Earth-type crops. Without antibiotics we'll starve! So we licensed a privateer. You see, with a pirate in action hereabouts and interstellar trade cut to ribbons, trading ships don't come to us. But there are some things we have to have. So our privateer

stops ships and requisitions goods, and we pay for them
with what we can, later. It's an emergency."

Trent said courteously, "Hmmmmm."

"This morning," she added, "when the pirate showed on
our detectors, we put on full drive to avoid it like any other
ship. But it overhauled us and closed in. We tried to dodge
and twist away, but it finally got close and blew our overdrive and we were helpless. We broke out of overdrive when
the blow-up came, and there was the pirate. And it said,
'*Commissioned privateer* Bear, *of Loren, calling. What ship's
that?*' "

The *Hecla*'s skipper took over the tale, fiercely. "I said,
'The devil you say! This is the *Hecla*, and Miss Hale's
aboard! You're going to find yourselves in trouble!' "

The girl interpolated, "It did look exactly like the *Bear!*"
Trent held up his hand. "Just a moment! You were hailed
by the pirate, pretending to be the *Bear*, which I understand is a privateer."

The girl nodded. "Yes. That's right."

"And you were not upset? Oh, I see now. The *Hecla* is
registered as owned on Loren. You were stopped by a ship
claiming to be a privateer from Loren. Naturally, you didn't
expect to be looted by a privateer from your home world. Is
that the way of it?"

The girl nodded again. She was horribly tense. She'd
known complete despair only a little while ago. She wore,
now, a very fine air of composure. But her hands were
clenched tightly. She seemed not to be aware of it. She was
trying hard to keep her lips from quivering. Trent approved
of her.

"And you," he turned to the *Hecla*'s skipper, "were so
sure you'd nothing to fear that you told this pirate that he
was going to get into trouble. You thought it was the *Bear*,
and it had stopped you."

"And blown our drive," said the skipper. "Of course I
thought he'd get into trouble! Miss Hale was aboard!"

"And—"

"The man at the pirate's communicator laughed. He laughed! And then we knew what had happened, and we tried to run away, and they followed and headed us off again and again. Finally they began to fire on us. Then a shell went into our engine room so we couldn't even try to run away any more."

Trent could picture it very clearly. The *Hecla*, plump and matronly and informed of coming doom, would have tried desperately to postpone the inevitable by crazy, panicky flight. The pirate followed. Perhaps for amusement it would have headed off the clumsy merchantman until that diversion palled. On the whole, it would have been very much like a man chasing a chicken or a pig when the time for it to die arrived. It would be horrible! In any case the pirate had put shells into the *Hecla* to drain her of air, and one shell hit the engine room and stopped the Lawlor drive, and then sent boats to take over. The pirates might have been admitted by airlock to commit their murders. Some people will coöperate most docilely with their intending killers, merely to get a few minutes more of life. Otherwise the pirates would have blasted a hole in their helpless victim's hull and entered through that.

Trent could picture it very clearly, from information about similar events elsewhere.

"And then we arrived," he observed.

"Nothing can ever repay you," said Marian warmly. "I . . . I've never really believed that anything dreadful could really happen to me. But it could, and it almost did. And you rescued me. So I . . . want to thank you."

"You've done it very nicely," said Trent, "but we haven't reached Sira yet. We might still run into trouble. Let me say that you're very welcome and let it go at that. Meanwhile, why don't you take over my cabin and rest up and get relaxed? You've had a pretty unpleasant experience.

She smiled at him and went out. The *Hecla*'s skipper followed her. Trent turned back to the instrument board. He looked at the detector dial with special care.

The *Yarrow*'s mate said dourly, "Captain, sir, no matter how it turned out, that was a bad fix for us to be in!"

"Yes," agreed Trent drily. "One should never take the owners' word about gadgets. I didn't like the affair, either. But if the fact means anything to you, we're heroes."

"It don't mean anything to me," said the mate bluntly.

"Then next time," said Trent, "we won't be heroic. Next time we run into pirates, we'll just let them cut our throats without any fuss."

But after the encounter, the effect of assured isolation produced a sort of coziness. The ship felt safe. Beautifully safe. Its air apparatus functioned perfectly. Its temperature control was set so that different parts of the occupied parts of the ship were at different degrees of heat or trivial chill, which made it feel somehow more natural. There were differences in smell. There were even growing plants in a suitable compartment. And the crewmen stood their watches placidly, and those off-watch loafed and gossiped.

But there was, at this moment, a spot illimitably removed from the *Yarrow* where a ship cut its overdrive and broke out back to normal space. Starlight shone on it. Its bow plates were dented and buckled. The forward third of its hull was airless, and no man could go there save through emergency airlocks between compartments, and they would die immediately if without a spacesuit. This was, of course, the ship that had called itself the *Bear* when summoning the *Hecla* to surrender.

The pirate's ship's company was not only raging but desperate. There were fewer crewmen than before it hailed the *Hecla*. When air left the forward third of its hull, there'd been men there without spacesuits on. In theory they'd had thirteen seconds in which to get into space-armor. None of them had made it. Nobody has ever made it. The surviving part of the crew wanted horribly to take revenge for the *Yarrow*'s act of self-defense.

But at the moment, the crew of the pirate ship labored with oxyhydrogen torches to repair the damage done by the *Yarrow*'s ramming attack. Extensive if temporary repairs were necessary for anything like normal operation of the ship that had named itself the *Bear*. But even after repair this ship couldn't go to a spaceport and there pass itself off as an innocent merchantman. Repairs couldn't be made in space that wouldn't need to be explained on ground. And it was very likely that the whole matter of the *Hecla*'s crippling would be known all through the Pleiads and elsewhere as fast as the news could travel.

In short, if before this event the pirate had ever passed in any spaceport as an honest craft about its lawful occasions, it couldn't do so any longer.

There was just one possibility. The *Hecla* had been disabled and hulled. Very probably, if the meddling *Yarrow* had the nerve to stand by to take off its crew, it was abandoned. But if the pirate ship could recover the *Hecla*—

The *Yarrow* drove for Sira. And Trent made tentative plans, tentatively allowing for what he thought the pirate might possibly do. If any of his guesses should turn out to be right, the pirates would most ferociously resent it.

III

MARIAN HALE WATCHED out a viewport while the great globe of Sira swelled and grew gigantic through the *Yarrow* approach. The *Hecla*'s skipper pointed out one of the three moons as the ship went past and explained what a Trojan orbit was. Later he pointed out landmarks on the enlarging world of Sira.

Eventually the ship touched ground. The girl, smiling, turned to Trent.

"We're aground, and there was a time when it didn't seem we'd ever be aground again! What are you going to do, Captain?"

"It's nearly noon here," said Trent. "Before sunset I'll have to do a little trading and I've some personal chores. Then I'll lift off again."

"When?"

"As soon as possible," he told her. "I'm not here for fun."

"I need to get in touch with our business agent," she observed. "We don't have ambassadors, here in the Pleiads, just business agents. Don't you think I'll be perfectly safe going on to Loren from here?"

He shrugged. He wasn't sure. There'd been one pirate ship, certainly, and while it wasn't likely to be professionally active again for a certain length of time, there might be more pirates in this area. There would be, to be sure, ships taking to space in the belief that the *Yarrow* had struck a hard blow at piracy. But that would make the time ripe for pirates to make many and rich captures.

"I'm not qualified to advise you. I'd say no, though I'm lifting off myself. If I were your father, I'd tell you to stay safely aground here until there'd been no ship missing for a good many months."

She smiled again. She held out her hand. He took it.

"I go aground now. Thank you, Captain. I have to help the *Hecla*'s crew report her loss and the circumstances. But you'll need to make a report too, won't you?"

He nodded. She didn't withdraw her hand.

"One thing more. Could you talk to our business agent for a few moments this afternoon before you lift off?"

"I'll try," said Trent.

He shook her hand formally, and she withdrew it. Again smiling, she went out of the control room and to ground. Trent, frowning, saw her walk to the spaceport offices. It was midday, here. It took thought to keep days and nights straight after a long time in space. Marian would rate as a very important person on Sira. Trent could bask briefly in the radiance of her importance if he chose. But he didn't.

He said briskly to the mate, "I'll have to talk about the *Hecla* at the spaceport office. Then I'll talk to some brokers, about our cargo. Then I'll take a look around the spaceport dives to see what kind of men are grounded here because of the pirates."

"Any ground leave for our men?" asked the mate.

28

"Hmm," said Trent. He considered. "Spaceport hands will take care of any cargo unloading I may arrange. But I'll lose time talking about the *Hecla*. Give them eight hours. We ought to be ready to lift off then."

"They'll just have time to get drunk," said the mate dourly, "and not enough to sober up again."

"I'm going to ship some extra hands if I can," Trent told him.

He turned to leave the control room. The mate said, "Captain?"

"What?"

"That lady," said the mate stolidly, "got to talk to me yesterday. She wanted to find out something. I didn't know whether to tell her or not."

"What did she want to know?"

"If you was married. I told her no. Right?"

"Yes," said Trent. "It's true. I'm not."

He went off the ship and to the very tedious business of answering questions about the *Hecla*, and then talking business to brokers and merchants gathered at the airport since news of a trading ship's arrival spread. They were very hungry for goods to sell. He parted with as much of his cargo as he thought wise. It was close to sundown before he went to investigate the places of business just outside the spaceport gates.

He applied for clearance to lift off at once. He had ten new hard-bitten characters to add to the *Yarrow*'s crew, and the ship was set to sail.

"*All hands prepare for lift,*" said Trent's voice from dozens of speakers, making a choral effect of the words. "*Lift starts in ten seconds. All hands to duty stations. Five seconds . . . Lift starts.*"

The *Yarrow* rose toward the star-filled night sky, and the lattice girders of the landing-grip slid past and vanished below. The planet Sira appeared as merely a vast blackness in which infinitesimal specks of light—street lamps—grew more and more minute until they disappeared. Then there was merely blackness against an inconceivable mass of stars.

But presently the sunlit part of Sira came into view and everything was changed.

The trading ship *Yarrow* went into overdrive after leaving Sira, and Trent had a sound night's sleep, and next ship-morning he was a good many million, billion, and trillion miles from it.

He went over the ship and found everything to his liking. Even McHinny showed him his pirate-discourager approaching re-completion. It was three-quarters of the way back into operating condition. Trent, feeling kindly to all the cosmos, praised him enough for McHinny to look almost contented. The new members of the crew had been put to work—the mate saw to that—and they regarded Trent with satisfying respect and confidence.

Trent himself worked painstakingly in the control room on a problem in mathematics. It was tricky. He wanted to re-locate the *Hecla*. The *Yarrow's* taped log had a record of all courses, drive strengths, and durations of drive since her departure from her home port. She could get back approximately to where she'd left the *Hecla*. But the *Hecla* wasn't there now.

She'd been sent off on her Lawlor drive on a course Trent had noted down. But real accuracy of position in space was out of the question. And nobody could tell what was accurate, anyhow. An attempt at it involved the local sun's proper motion—the sun from whose system one had started out—one's individual velocity in three dimensions due to the motion of the spaceport one left, a highly corrected account of drive efficiency, the total mass of ship and cargo, and a few score other factors.

And, starting from that, there was the problem of finding the *Hecla*. In the end Trent calculated a cone of probability. The *Hecla* should be within that imaginary geometrical shape in space. Her most probable position would be somewhere along its axis. As one went out from it the probability would grow less. And the *Hecla* would be still accelerating.

He did the best he could and went to see how the combat instructions went on. They went well. He added some details.

One of the new hands made a suggestion. It was a good one. He incorporated it into the course of instruction. It looked more and more as if he were preparing for a piratical career. On the second day out of port he suspended the weapons exercises to shift cargo. He had masses of relatively low-value cargo packed in the *Yarrow*'s bow. The reason was, of course, that the pirate had carried and used a gun. Trent had seen one of the projectiles, spent, in the *Hecla*'s engine room. It had penetrated the *Hecla*'s inner and outer hulls, but had done little damage inside. He shifted cargo so that a shell from dead ahead would have to pierce not only the *Yarrow*'s two hulls but various bales of merchandise before it could do much damage. The understanding was, naturally, that the *Yarrow* would be driving toward any cannon-carrying antagonist in any action that took place.

The mate nodded stolidly when Trent explained it.

"If I'm not aboard," said Trent, "it may be a good trick."

The mate nodded again, but he didn't really grasp the idea that Trent might be missing from the *Yarrow* and himself in command. He didn't even grasp it when, entering the hand-written items in the control room log—quite separate from the engine room taped record—he found a memo in Trent's handwriting:

"11-4-65 8 *bells dog. According to agreement owners* Yarrow *now engaged salvage at charter rate until return commercial port.*"

It was very conscientious of Trent.

Four days passed. Five. Six. Trent brought the *Yarrow* out of overdrive. The stars were a very welcome sight. He sent out an emergency radar pulse. One. He waited half an hour. Nothing came back. In overdrive, he shifted the *Yarrow*'s position. Again he sent out a radar pulse.

It was unpleasant. Everybody on the *Yarrow* experienced the sensations accompanying a switch into or out of overdrive twice every half-hour. Presently everybody's belly-muscles ached from the knotted cramps that came with the nausea every time.

On some ships, under some skippers, there would have

been protests right away. On the *Yarrow* under Trent there were no protests, but there were pained questions about how long it would be kept up.

"I'm looking for something," said Trent pleasantly. "When I find it, this will stop."

The inquiring crewman was satisfied, if unhappy. He spread the word among the rest. There were guesses at what Trent might be looking for. There was general agreement that it must be a ship, of whose course and probable position Trent had information. But granting that, the guesses ranged from a space liner chartered to carry colonists, including women, to their new homes, down to a mere bank ship carrying rare metals to balance financial accounts between star clusters. But nobody guessed at the *Hecla*.

It was the *Hecla*, though. Naturally! But the return of a radar pulse came only after many surges of radar radiation following the crewman's question.

Then the radar pulse did come back, and the *Yarrow* moved toward the reflection point. This, obviously, had to be in normal space, with stars. In terms of miles traveled, the pursuit of the distant object was trivial. But Trent had not only to overtake it but to match velocities. It was a rather painful operation, but in time it was accomplished. The *Hecla* floated alongside the *Yarrow*, presently, and Trent leaped the space between the big steel hulls. Arrived, he crawled along the *Hecla*'s hull to the open airlock door through which he'd left it many days before. He swung in and released his lifeline. The lock door closed. In minutes the *Hecla* ceased to accelerate and the *Yarrow* shot ahead and the mate had to bring her back around and come alongside again.

Then there was fine and finicky maneuvering. Ultimately the two ships touched gingerly. Cargo doors opened, facing each other. Cargo from the *Yarrow* went aboard the wrecked *Hecla*. Men went about the inside of that ship, searching for the places where solid-shot missiles had penetrated. Some of them were to be stopped, not all. There was violent activity of other sorts. Tanks of air went from one ship to the other, police equipment bought on Dorade, Shaped-charge explosive packages, satchel-bombs, food and water.

Trent went back aboard the *Yarrow* for final consultation with the mate.

"You'll head for Sira," he commanded. "We didn't make delivery of everything I agreed to sell on Sira. You can finish up with that. Then you can go on to Manaos. Here are some cargo lists and prices. You can unload this stuff for these prices. Understand?"

The mate nodded.

"If all goes well," Trent told him, "I'll come into port on Manaos. You can wait for me there for three weeks. Then if you like you can hunt for me along here." He indicated an area on a three-dimensional chart of this part of the Pleiad cluster. "If you don't find us in a reasonable time go back to Manaos. Maybe we'll have made it. If we aren't there then, you're the *Yarrow's* skipper. In which case, look out for Mc-Hinny. He means well but he's a fool. Don't ever take his advice!"

The mate nodded again. He looked acutely unhappy.

Presently the *Yarrow* drew away from the *Hecla*. That round-bellied cargo-carrier of space looked intact. It wasn't. Its overdrive coil was blown and its Lawlor drive patched for strictly emergency use. It was empty of air and there were shell-holes in its plating.

The *Yarrow* went into overdrive. It vanished. The *Hecla* was left alone.

In a way, it was curiously like the occasion when a barkentine of an earlier time had been found by an earlier Captain Trent, battered by cannon balls and leaking, with its masts shot overside and its boats long gone. This was in a sea where Captain Trent was bitterly unwelcome, so much so that a man-of-war had been assigned especially to hunt for him. But he went aboard the derelict with hands from his proper crew, and his proper ship sailed away leaving him to make what he could of the situation.

It was quite a similar state of things, except that the Captain Trent of the *Yarrow* was aboard a derelict of space, and the ship that wanted ferociously to find him was a pirate.

It was now very nearly ready to resume its professional activities.

IV

THERE WERE NO oxyhydrogen torches to be burned for the refitting of the *Hecla* for space. There was nothing for incurious stars to see. Mere plastic sealings would have closed the shot-holes in her double hull, but Trent forbade it for the time being. Every other repair went smoothly. There was no reason for spaceboats to stir in the metal blisters which were their proper repositories. There was no particular reason for anything at all, in the way of visible repairwork, to be performed upon the fabric of the *Hecla*. She lay seemingly motionless in that emptiness and quietude and remoteness which is between-the-stars. That extra air tanks had been taken aboard, and tools, and food and water and certain eccentric equipment designed for planetary police forces; that these things, formerly absent, were now present in the *Hecla's* hull could not be discovered from outside it. The *Hecla* lay still, matronly, clumsy, bewilderedly acquiescent in her doom. The stars regarded her without interest or curiosity.

Trent sealed off certain areas inside the ship, filled them with air from the ship's reserves, and put his new recruits to the rewinding of the overdrive coil. He himself made a good repair to an emergency-patched cable in the Lawlor drive casing. Also, with painstaking care he set the tape-recorded log to register such actions as took place after the *Hecla's* reoccupation.

It wasn't on the whole a very difficult business. Hundreds of ships had blown their overdrive coils and rewound them in space and gone sedately on about their lawful occasions.

Thousands had had trouble with their Lawlor drives, but like all superlatively difficult achievements the design of those useful engines was so blessedly simple that nobody felt incapable of the work that would make them whole and functioning again.

Trent did do a certain amount of stage dressing, though. His crew for the *Hecla*, recruited on Sira, had cherished very unusual hopes. They expected high excitement out here, and it would have been anticlimactic to set them at a far from routine but by no means hazardous salvage operation. So Trent dressed it up.

He let only the parts of the ship necessary for the repair of the drives and a reasonable living space be refilled with air. Most of the ship remained empty, with shot holes unplugged. He painstakingly led his followers, two by two and in spacesuits, through the less frequently visited and now airless parts of the ship. They came to know their way about the bilges, through all the air-seal doorways, until they were able to move from any part of the ship to any other without appearing in the regularly used areas. And he had them carry small arms on these occasions.

It was largely stage dressing, but not wholly that. Trent still had to think of possibilities. He was not exactly certain that the pirate which had wrecked the *Hecla* was itself destroyed. He prepared against the possibility that it was not, by charming his crewmen with prospects of lurid action. They learned and rehearsed battle tactics and in so doing prepared to be attacked. If the pirate ship should appear, Trent and his followers were prepared. If it didn't, nevertheless he'd keep up the continual alert until he brought the *Hecla* to ground again, and then a reasonable bonus for work done and danger undergone would satisfy everybody. He'd be under no obligation to explain his precautions once they'd ended.

There were personal angles to the matter, too. He'd taken Marian Hale out of a very unpleasant situation. But there is something about the relationship between men and women which obligates a man who's done a woman one favor to do her another and another indefinitely. Trent had meant to salvage the *Hecla* from the moment of the pirate's disappearance in overdrive, when the *Hecla* was left helpless in space. If Marian had been another man, even the *Hecla*'s owner, Trent could have admitted his intentions frankly or even discussed the method and the practicability of the job. But once he'd taken Marian from the wrecked *Hecla,* if they advanced to a state of cordial friendship he'd be under an obligation to do her the second favor of doing the salvage for at most the cost of the operation, because it belonged to her father. The fact was illogical but it was still a fact.

One shipday passed. Another, and another. The rewinding of the overdrive coil went along at a steady pace. Partly as stage-dressing, to be sure, but also with sound reason, Trent kept men watching certain dials every minute of every shipday and night. The *Hecla*'s radar remained unoperated. Its pulses could be recognized for what they were. Her overdrive field detector was definitely not in use. It could be detected at many times a radar's effective range. But he did have radar-frequency listening devices turned up to maximum gain. They should give notice instantly if anybody hit the *Hecla* with even a single radar pulse, such as Trent had used to find it when a derelict.

Stars and nebulae and galaxies shone all about the interior of a seeming hollow sphere whose center was apparently the spaceship. That slightly over-plump vessel showed no faintest sign of life. She floated in emptiness. That was all. If watched from a fixed position—which could not exist where she lay between the stars—her bow might have been seen to wander vaguely to various headings. But that had no significance at all. There was absolutely nothing about the *Hecla* which could have told another vessel at a hundred yards' distance that she was alive.

But Trent worried about whether or not he ought to worry. There was no way for him to know. If the pirate survived at all, it was either badly damaged or it was not. If badly damaged, he needn't worry. If not, the damage would either make her head for her base, or not. If the pirate headed for her base, he needn't worry. If not, she'd either hunt for a ship she'd already disabled—the *Hecla*—or not. If she didn't hunt for the *Hecla*, he needn't disturb himself. If she did, she'd either find the *Hecla* or not. And if she did she could lie off at a distance and pound that already-battered ship with solid shot until no possible life or chance for life remained. And she would.

So it was with concern that he heard the spaceman on radar watch say uncertainly, "Cap'n sir, it looked to me like a radar pulse hit us just now. But it was only the one."

Trent took a deep breath.

"That's the way it would be. Watch for another." He spoke into the microphone of the all-hands speaker system. "All hands! All hands! We've got company coming. All hands clean ship. Tidy up. Everything from Sira down in the bilges. Suits on."

There began a stirring everywhere; men moved or labored throughout the ship. Some donned spacesuits immediately and then set about an elaborate tidying process. Some swept floors before donning space armor. Others carried small arms and ammunition out of sight. Men struggled with extra air tanks and with food and water containers brought here in the *Yarrow*. Police equipment Trent had bought on Dorade many weeks ago was hidden. His new crewmen were thoroughly familiar with it.

Trent went to the engine room where the rewinding of the overdrive coil went on. He estimated the amount remaining to be done.

He said wrily, "If they'd only held off for two more hours!"

The man on radar-watch called from the engine room, "*Cap'n, another pulse! Somebody's headin' this way!*"

"They would be," said Trent distastefully. To the men in the engine room he added, "Keep on winding, but have your suits ready. Make it as quick as you can. This is nasty!"

He made a circuit of the ship, while men watched him expectantly. One man asked hopefully, "D'you know who's coming, sir?"

"It's the pirate, I hope," said Trent peevishly. "The one

who's been sniping ships all through the Pleiads. Maybe there's more than one. If so, this is the one that wrecked the *Hecla*. And it's coming and we're not ready for it!" Then he said sharply, "Look at that! That doesn't look like an empty ship. Get it out of sight!"

Somebody bundled up blankets that had been spread on the floor for dice to be rolled on. It wouldn't have been in use by the crew of a properly operating ship, so they wouldn't have left it behind when they left.

"Open the port lock door," commanded Trent. "That's the way it was left. Nothing untidy, now! Then get all weapons ready, pick your spots, and use gas if you can."

There were scurryings and more scurryings. Men elatedly completed the completely unusual task of making an occupied, worked-in spaceship look like it had been abandoned a long while back and never reoccupied. Much of the ship didn't need attention. Trent had only put air into the compartments necessary for the repair of the Lawlor drive and the overdrive coil, plus a reasonable living space.

Another call from the control room. *"Another radar pulse, sir! Pretty strong!"*

"All hands in suits," commanded Trent. He'd ordered it before. To the two men still winding the coil he said irritably, "We're going to bleed out all the air. Work in your spacesuits as long as you can. Then get out of sight!"

He checked each spaceman separately, emphasizing that all suit-microphones must be switched to "OFF." Reception, though, was desirable. Then he went to the control room. There he could watch through the viewports and see what the approaching ship did. The *Hecla*, of course, was no better armed than she'd been when first halted. Her overdrive was still inoperable until the winding was finished, and if and when it could be used, the pirate should be able to blow it instantly. Trent released all the air from what parts of the ship were air-filled. The ship became airless, like the derelict it represented itself to be.

Then he waited.

SPACE CAPTAIN

There is only one set of circumstances in which a man in the control room of one ship between the stars ever sees another. Normally, ships in deep space are in overdrive and moving too fast to be sighted even if their overdrive fields allowed it. It is not even possible for two ships to rendezvous more than a few hundred million miles from a marker such as a star. Observations taken down to a second of arc are simply not precise enough to bring them within detection range of one another. The only way in which one spaceship can actually sight another is when by assisted chance one ship detects the overdrive of a second and closes in on it instead of the conventional swerving away. If it can get close enough, guided by the overdrive detector, one of the two overdrive coils will blow. Then the unharmed other ship can break out to normal space and join the first one there by tracking it down by radar. But this process happens to be congenial only to pirates and privateers. Honest merchant ships refrain from using it.

But, Trent, in the *Hecla's* control room in very deep space, saw another ship.

First it was radar pulses coming from nowhere and with decreasing intervals between. Then it was something which made a single star on a vision screen wink out for the fraction of a second, and then another and another and still others. Then it was a glittering. And then it was a shape moving swiftly closer and growing in size as it did so.

The *Hecla's* communicator-speaker bellowed and Trent's helmet picked it up by induction. There was no air in the control room to carry sound. There was no air anywhere, except in her reserve tanks.

"What ship's that?"

Trent naturally did not reply. The call was repeated.

"What ship's that?" rasped the voice from the other ship. *"Answer or take what you'll get! We'll put some shells into you!"*

Trent waited. He didn't expect bombardment. It would be rather futile. He felt a certain detached anticipation which, had he known about it, would have been interestingly similar

39

to the reactions of an ancestor of his some centuries before. That other Captain Trent had a half-keg of gunpowder beside him, and when the moment was just right he'd touch a slow-match to its fuse and drop it into the midst of an approaching body of men who'd arrogantly forced their way into a place where they didn't belong. He, also, waited in a peculiarly detached calm.

But the Captain Trent of the *Yarrow* and the *Hecla* had longer to wait. The other ship came nearer and Trent saw what only previous victims of this particular ship had ever exactly seen. He saw the pirate in the light of between-the-stars. It had been sleek and somehow it was still deadly to look at.

It circled the *Hecla*, and he saw welds and patches on its outer bow-plating. It was definitely the ship the *Yarrow* had rammed, repaired in space by men who deserved credit for that achievement. But they were not otherwise to be admired.

It circled again. It could see the *Hecla*'s port-side airlock door left open. No ship which was occupied would have an airlock open to space. But if a ship was abandoned, the last man to leave it would hardly bother to close such a door behind him.

It was convincing. The pirate came to an apparent stop a half mile off. It appeared to drift backward, and then that drift was over-corrected, and it was a long time before the two ships floated almost exactly still in relation to each other.

Then lifeboat blisters opened their mussel-shell-shaped covers. Two spaceboats came out and moved toward the *Hecla*. Trent murmured into his phone. It wouldn't go outside the ship.

"Boats approaching," he said curtly. "I won't be able to use this helmet-phone after they board us, or their helmets will pick it up. Stand by to carry out orders when I give the word."

Silence. Then clankings. Trent heard them by solid conduction as he made his way along those un-obvious passages in the bilges which he and all his crewmen had already memorized. He touched his helmet to a metal wall. Yes. A spaceboat had tied up to the open airlock. He heard metal-soled boots on the airlock floor. Men came into the ship. The lock worked again, though there was no air for it to keep imprisoned. More men came in. The second spaceboat was lying a little way off until the first should report all clear.

Trent remained perfectly still, listening. He was in a narrow passageway by which the *Hecla*'s cargo holds could be by-passed. He heard men tramping all over the ship: the control room—airless; the engine room—airless. The men who'd been rewinding the overdrive coil were gone, of course. They'd left the coil looking as if no hand had touched it since it blew—its metal case was still bulged and discolored from heat—but they were only behind the engine room sidewall. The pirate crewmen went into the living quarters. They were airless too, and they'd been swept and garnished so that they looked exactly as the *Hecla* had looked when it was a full-powered, fully manned and fully loaded ship of space, complacently speeding from one world to another. But then, of course, her hull had been full of air.

There were voices in Trent's helmet-phones. Men reported the ship empty. One man went to the airlock to open its outer door so his spacephone message could be picked up by the nearby pirate ship. Somebody'd tried to use the ship's space-communication equipment to call the pirate, waiting half a mile away. But there was no air to carry sound to its micro-phone.

"Maybe a shell cut a wire," said an authoritative voice. *"No,"* said another voice. *"No air."* Yet another voice said, *"No passengers either."* Then various voices reported, *"All clear aft." "Nobody aboard." "All set. I think there's a little air aft, but I'm not sure."*

The authoritative voice said; *"Some air aft? See if you can build up pressure. Maybe there're no shot-holes aft."*

Listening tranquilly, Trent found that the interior of the ship sounded like a very busy place. Men moved here and there and everywhere, exchanging comments by space-phone, but there was no cause for suspicion. The comments ceased to be about the condition of the ship and became comments on the apparent luxury and riches of the food supply, and the practically bulging cargo holds, and so on.

The authoritative voice said, *"Call in the other boat. Have 'em tell the ship everything's all right except the communicator. That'll work when there's air."*

Trent stayed quite still, listening with a fine satisfaction as the second spaceboat made fast outside the airlock. The spacesuit tanks of his followers had a good two hours of air in them. He considered that he and they could remain completely out of sight while the pirate crewmen made free with the *Hecla*. And if the pirate came alongside to take on cargo, in a fine conviction that it had exclusive possession of the derelict *Hecla*. . . .

Unfortunately, it didn't work out that way. Within minutes of their boarding, the boarding party had proved past question that the *Hecla* was as empty of occupants as of air. There'd been no doubt about it to begin with. Things had to be that way! The second boatload of spacemen came stamping aboard through the airlock. The pirate crew—this more or less astonishing Trent—set about plugging the shot-holes their ship's gun had made, to restore the hull to air-tightness. It took a considerable time. Then they took air from the reserve tanks and filled the ship with it so the *Hecla* became re-filled with breathable air, icy, from its expansion from enormously high pressure to fourteen pounds to the square inch, but still very breathable. And then the men who believed that they were the new owners of the *Hecla* got cheerfully out of their spacesuits and began to examine their prize for objects of value. Some went to the cargo holds and began to smash open crates at random. That wouldn't have been really practical in space armor. Some searched the passenger quarters. They were disappointed in the loot found there, though, because by their own doing traffic in the Pleiads had been cut by ninety per cent, and passenger traffic by more than that. But the authoritative voice growled at them. It named two men and commanded them to the engine room. They were to examine the overdrive coil in detail. Moreover, they were to see what damage had been done to the Lawlor-drive unit.

Waiting and listening, Trent was moved to swear. He'd had high hopes. But anybody who uncovered the overdrive coil could see that it was almost rewound. A glance at the Lawlor engine would show that it had been worked on recently. The order meant that the pirates didn't intend merely to loot and abandon the ship, but to make use of it. Perhaps to change into it!

There was only one thing to be done. He spoke into the helmet-phone. His followers could hear it. The pirates out of space armor wouldn't. He turned on his spacephone and said, *"Let's go!"*

Then he appeared suddenly in the living quarters, where two of the pirates jumped visibly and plunged away in the panic of men who have put off their weapons with their spacesuits and are faced by a man who hasn't. Trent used a police weapon. It was necessary for him and his followers to be victors in the ambush they'd made. So when Trent pushed down the triggers of the gas-pistols at his belt, they didn't emit flames or thermite bullets. They flung out clouds of thick fog-gas, mixed to exactly the most efficient combination of dense fog laced with sneeze- and tear-gas. Which nobody could defy.

Those two pirates went down and kicked and jerked in convulsive sneezings they had no power to stop. Their eyes streamed tears. Trent felt a queasy disappointment. They were pirates, and they specifically would have murdered Marian as they'd murdered enough others. But instead of being captured in proper battle, he'd trapped them like rats and they were as unharmed and as helpless as petty criminals in the hands of planetary police.

"How's it going?" asked Trent in his space-helmet.

There was a crash, and a grunting voice said with pleasure, *"Not bad! That one's out!"*

There were other noises, confused ones. Trent, angry to profanity, heard the sound of running feet transmitted by the material of a spacesuit to the microphone inside its helmet. He could tell that the wearer of the spacesuit transmitting was plunging in pursuit. Another voice said zestfully, *"He's mine!"* Then somewhere else—he could only tell by the different timber of the voices—a man swore and panted, *"Y'would, would you!"* And there was a harsh noise, and after that only pantings. But somewhere a deadly weapon rasped, and there was roaring, and he knew that a compartment somewhere was flooded with fog-gas, and that a man who tried to kill with an ordinary instrument for murder was now seized by his own body and made to sneeze and sneeze as he tried with tearing eyes to find another target in the vapor all around him. And Trent heard the weapon fall as further monstrous convulsions of sneezing tore at him.

It was a singularly disappointing conflict. Trent's disappointment was marked among his followers, too. They'd trained and practiced and labored to acquire skill in combat in the steel-plate jungle of a spaceship's least-used parts. They could, they believed, fight ten times their number in this special area of battle, and come out victorious. But instead they'd used ground-police fog-gas, designed for the suppression of riots, and they felt no greater triumph than comes of using an exterminator's spray to be rid of unpleasant insects.

They brought the pirate crewmen, still suffering paroxysms of sneezing, and contemptuously piled them in a heap because they'd been so ingloriously subdued. Later they bound them, without even that unwilling respect a man will give to a sneak-thief who fights bitterly when he's seized.

"Now," said Trent precisely, "there's the pirate ship. Keep your suits on. We got these characters because they made themselves comfortable. We don't want that for ourselves. Heave them in some small compartment and weld the door shut on them. We've got to get away from their ship."

He scowled. Things hadn't gone as he planned. He'd hoped to bring his crewmen out of the bilges after the pirate and the *Hecla* were lashed to each other for the transfer of cargo. He'd looked for a total surprise and the possible capture of the pirate ship by boarding—a boarding-party appearing from nowhere, deadly in the sort of fighting the pirates had never bothered to learn.

One of his crewmen said ruefully by helmet-phone, *"It wasn't much of a fuss, Cap'n. Shall we go back to work on the overdrive coil?"*

For a long time the two ships lay in space with barely half a mile between them. Nothing visibly happened. The *Hecla's* nose pointed successively to an eighth-magnitude star and then to a dim red speck of light halfway to the Milky Way, and then to a fairly bright green one. The wanderings of its axis among far-away and unconcerned suns had no significance. The pirate ship accompanied it in its drifting. The men left in it waited impatiently for the prize-crew to report repairs on the way and some idea of what cargo the *Hecla* carried. Then it would decide whether to send the *Hecla* to its base with a minimum crew, or take what cargo was worth taking and leave the ship a derelict.

But the information didn't come. The pirate ship called by communicator. There was no answer. It called again. No reply. The boats had reported that all was as anticipated and their crews had entered the *Hecla.* There'd been a further report or two from them. But now there were no more reports. The pirate waited impatiently.

Stars looked down from overhead, and up from the immeasurable abyss below, and gazed abstractedly from every other direction. The pirate ship called yet again. And again. Two-thirds of what crew it had left was aboard the *Hecla.* They'd reported all well. The crewmen still aboard the pirate were now merely a skeleton crew, because they'd lost men in the ripped-open compartments from the ramming, and most of the rest had boarded the *Hecla.* The ship couldn't afford to send more men to find out why they didn't answer its calls. The *Hecla* was theirs. It was captured and occupied. But it didn't answer calls!

The reaction on the pirate ship wasn't exactly rage. It was mostly pure, stark, superstitious bewilderment. This couldn't happen! Minute after minute, quarter-hour after quarter-hour, the pirate ship called frantically to its boarding-party in the *Hecla*.

Then, quite suddenly, there were swirlings and clouds and jets and outpourings of vapor from the *Hecla*. She seemed to become the center of an utterly impossible cloud of vapor. It almost hid her. There were flashes and explosions in this starlit preposterousness.

And then the *Hecla* vanished.

V

IN THE UNWRITTEN history of the family line of Captains Trent, there was no other achievement which exactly matched this. It was because, of course, no exactly similar problem had ever turned up before. The *Hecla* was unarmed save for such equipment as even a small-town police department might possess. But with it Trent had managed to drive away from the repaired pirate ship with more than half its original crew in captivity aboard, without pursuit by the pirate, and without even an injury to any of his own spacemen. And he was disappointed because he'd hoped to capture the pirate ship itself.

The vapor he'd used was, of course, all the fog-gas-contaminated air in the ship, released at once with more fog-gas poured into the outgoing flood. The flashes were tear-gas bombs exploded outside the ship on the side away from the pirate. And the vanishing of the *Hecla* was simply her rewound overdrive coil in action, with the repaired Lawlor drive pushing at capacity to make use of it while the pirate still desperately tried to make contact with its boarding-parties.

The final element the pirate could not understand was the vapor. Gases released in space fling themselves precipitately in all directions toward nothingness. But here was a cloud in space. And the answer they didn't think of was that fog-gas was not a vapor but a suspension of ultra-microscopic particles, which do not repel each other with the vehemence of gas particles.

So the pirate ship lay stunned and bewildered, contemplating the vapor-cloud where the *Hecla* had been as it slowly spread and thinned and finally disappeared.

That cloud, obviously, was more stage-setting. Your normal criminal is a very practical person, but timid. He is deeply suspicious of things he does not understand, and Trent had arranged a series of events that would be wholly mystifying to anybody who hadn't seen the preparations to bring them about. Trent's stage-dressing mystified the pirate skipper, and by the time—stammering and frustrated and with his mind effectively scrambled—by the time he looked at the overdrive detector to see if the *Hecla* had vanished in overdrive, Trent had made a full-velocity overdrive dash while confusion in the pirate's control room could be counted on. By the time the pirate's detector was examined, he was some thousands of overdrive miles away but in normal space again, listening for a possible radar-pulse. By the time the pirate attempted that, for an explanation of no drivefield registering on his instruments, Trent was back in overdrive on an entirely new course.

For a very considerable period, then, he alternated between time in and out of overdrive. For as long as the pirate stumblingly tried to follow, Trent ran the *Hecla* on a zig-zag pattern of tracks with which his ancestors in the last two wars on Earth were familiar. They'd used it to thwart submarines. Captain Trent of the *Yarrow* and the *Hecla* used it to elude a pirate.

It worked very well. In due time he made a planet-fall on the world of Manaos, and again in due time its landing-grid sent up fumbling, nudging fields of force, and they locked onto the *Hecla* and drew her down to ground.

And there Trent adopted the manners and customs of businessmen. He behaved with great sedateness. He reported

to the spaceport authorities that he'd brought in the salvaged
Hecla. She'd been attacked by pirates. A full account of the
event was on file on the planet Sira. She'd been abandoned
by her captain and crew because she was disabled, with her
overdrive and Lawlor units useless, her air gone, and the
return of the pirate to be anticipated. An account of this was
also on file on Sira. He, Trent, had found and salvaged her.
He resigned her now to the custody of the Admiralty Court
on Manaos, making due claim for salvage on the ship and her
cargo.

And then he mentioned negligently that he had twelve
members of the pirate's crew welded into an emptied cargo
hold, to whom food and water had been supplied through
small openings since their capture. He'd be glad to have them
taken off his hands. And then he asked if by any chance his
proper ship the *Yarrow* had come into port on Manaos.

She hadn't.

There was great enthusiasm on Manaos over the capture
of the pirates. An imposing array of police in ground-cars
and with copters flying overhead went to the spaceport to
receive them from Trent. There were mobs in the street to
observe the cavalcade. Other crowds tried to crash the
spaceport gate to watch as the police went into the *Hecla*
to remove the prisoners. Trent and his crewmen identified
them separately—they'd make formal depositions about them
later—and then let the police bring them out of the cargo
hold.

After nearly two weeks' imprisonment with no coddling,
the prisoners were not prepossessing. They were unshaven
and disheveled and repulsive. But above all they were de-
fiant.

Stridently and with fury, they announced to news cameras
that they would not be hanged. Their shipmates and their
ship's companion pirate vessels would be working from this
moment to gather hostages for their safety. They'd take tens of
dozens of spacemen and space travelers prisoner and hold
them. If anything happened to the captive pirates, much
more and worse would befall the prisoners the pirates would

take. The un-piratical Pleiad worlds could count, rasped the prisoners, on having not less than a dozen crewmen and passengers in space murdered for every pirate punished. There would be picture-tapes, presently, of the details of sample pirate captives being killed, to show precisely what would happen on a larger scale if Trent's captives were harmed.

These defiances, of course, were broadcast live to every vision-screen on the planet. Then small and very agile space craft took to space and vanished, bound for the other Pleiad worlds. They took with them the highest value in cargo such minute space craft could carry. It was news. They'd be paid so extravagantly for news that they felt the risk of themselves being captured by pirates was justified.

The twelve prisoners were carried by helicopter to an official prison, since their defiance meant danger to them if they were carried through the streets. Then police had to be posted about the *Hecla* to protect Trent from admirers and still more from newsmen.

He was practically besieged in the *Hecla* for three days. Then the cordon of camera-carrying watchers more or less diminished, because the *Hecla*'s salvage crew was at large upon the town and were much more exciting sources of news. They'd originally slipped out of the ship to spend their wages. But they found they couldn't. They were everywhere surrounded by admirers who wouldn't let them spend their money. People gloated because somebody had been victorious over a pirate ship, the victory consisting of escape from it and the use of police-type weapons upon a dozen of its crew. The men who'd salvaged the *Hecla* found that they had innumerable friends who wanted to buy them drinks and bask in their society. They even found themselves possessed of vast charm to the ladies they met about the spaceport. They told highly embroidered tales of pirates and piracy and deeds of derring-do, and everybody was convinced that the age of piracy was at an end.

Trent waited for the *Yarrow*. He found himself less popular than his crewmen. They, at least, said nothing discouraging to anybody. But Trent did. Asked for advice about ships taking to space again, he pointed out that he'd cost one pirate ship some men. That was all. There might be more than one pirate ship. He was inclined to think, he said curtly, that the planets of a given star-group should cooperate and establish something like an armed force to make piracy unprofitable. He didn't think that impractical, but he did not think that his own personal salvage of one ship the pirates had disabled justified anyone else in lifting off ground. Not yet.

His opinion was too sensible to make a good news story. In the first week after he brought the *Hecla* to ground, no less than three previously grounded ships left the Manaos spaceport to attempt business as usual but at higher prices among the stars. During the second week, four more left for emptiness. In the third week—when he was beginning to worry about the *Yarrow*—four more lifted off. The same thing was undoubtedly happening through the Pleiad group as the news of Trent's achievement spread.

He wasn't happy about it. When the *Yarrow* finally came into port, long after sundown and with the mate in command, the mate reported stolidly that he'd completed the trading deals Trent had arranged on Sira. He felt that he could have traded much more and at a higher profit but for the news that tiny news-carrying craft were spreading energetically through the Pleiads.

"All kinds of ships are lifting off," said the mate stolidly. "They're racing to try to hit high-priced markets with their merchandise. That Miss . . . Miss Hale, she took passage on the *Cytheria,* bound first to Midway and then to Loren. She left port the same day we did. There's a letter for you."

He handed it over. Trent read it. He swore despairingly.

Long ago and away back in the succession of Captains Trent, a certain Captain Trent, after due reflection, decided that he'd made a mistake about the young lady he'd just bidden a decorous good-bye to on the quarterdeck of a ship her father owned. Having reflected, he decided that she

shouldn't, after all, be allowed to return to a state of tute-
lage under her father. He was plainly not calculated to be a
good influence on her. He was not a fit companion for her.
He was positively not qualified to pass on so important a
matter as who should be the young lady's husband. And
having come to this conclusion, that Captain Trent immediately put out to sea to overtake her ship. Conservative persons
considered that he carried a hazardous amount of sail,
considering the weather. But it was rumored that he had permitted no delay for any purpose whatever except the loading
of his barkentine's guns.

This, however, was hardly a parallel to Trent's actions
now. His motivation was a polite and wholly decorous letter
from Marian Hale.

Dear Captain Trent;

*I've just heard of your marvellous achievement in re-taking
the* Hecla *from pirates who'd boarded her, and of coming
into port on Manaos with half the pirate crew in irons. I am
boasting that I know you personally! Please let me suggest,
though, that you let my father make a proposal in settlement
of salvage on the* Hecla. *It will certainly not be less to your
advantage than an Admiralty Court award, and the legal
expenses will be much less!*

I do hope you will bring the Hecla *to Loren in completion
of such an arrangement. I am anxious to have my father
thank you for me as I thank you for myself. Since you have
made the spaceways quite safe again, I am sailing for home
on the* Cytheria, *which will leave today and stop first at Midway and then go on to Loren. I do hope to introduce you to
my father. He owes you so much! And so do I.*

> *Sincerely,*
> *Marian Hale.*

Considered dispassionately, it was not a remarkable letter,
though it had cost much more effort and spoiled paper in
its composition than most. But Trent didn't read it dispassionately. Marian was in space. Now. And there were pirate

ships in space. He burst into explosive words at the next to last sentence. The *Yarrow*'s mate stared at him.

"I've sold some of the *Yarrow*'s cargo," said Trent feverishly, "but no money's passed, so that's all right. I'm going to get the *Yarrow* cleared for immediate lift-off for Loren. You get the small arms from the *Hecla* while I get clearance and a lift-off order." Then he said fiercely, "Don't let anything keep you from having those small arms on board and anything else you have to have by the time I'm back!"

He left the *Yarrow* and headed for the spaceport office practically at a run. As he ran, he swore bitterly. In a perfectly real sense it was not his business that Marian Hale took passage on a spaceship at a time he considered dangerous. It wasn't his business that ships lifted off from Manaos at the same time. But he'd brought Marian off the *Hecla* when by the laws of probability neither she nor any other member of the *Hecla*'s company should ever have been heard of again. He felt no responsibility for any of the *Hecla*'s crew even now. They could take care of themselves. But Marian couldn't. Trent had the extremely unhappy feeling that nobody but himself was qualified to protect Marian from disaster. He'd proved it. Now she very likely was heading for further disaster and again nobody but himself seemed to be qualified to do anything about it.

He reached the spaceport office, and it was more than two hours after sunset. There was a clerk on duty, to be sure, but he was on stand-by watch. He read placidly in an office chair placed in a good light. He looked up inquiringly when Trent came in the office door.

"Lift-off clearance," said Trent curtly. "The *Yarrow*. She came in an hour ago. I'm taking her out again. Make it fast!"

The clerk recognized Trent. There weren't many people on at least half a dozen planets of the Pleiads who wouldn't have recognized him today and tomorrow and probably the day after tomorrow. But fame is fleeting, and notoriety is more so, and Trent did not and wouldn't ever have that steady, recurrent, repetitive mention in the news tapes that would make anybody recall his name after three days of no public mention. But the clerk did recognize him tonight. He even tried to be obliging. But there was difficulty.

"The *Yarrow* came in under her mate," said the spaceport clerk uneasily, "and you want to take her out again as skipper. I know it's perfectly all right, Captain, but I can't order the grid operator to lift you off unless. . . ."

Trent exploded. The clerk looking almost frightened, set about the unsnarling of red tape. Trent paced up and down the office, muttering to himself, while a clerk made vision-phone calls, and located somebody who would have to sign something, and somebody else who would have to authorize something, and somebody else still who must put an official stamp on it. And Trent halted sometimes to listen to a particular conversation, and then began to pace again.

He did not think tenderly of Marian. He raged, because he had saved her once from a very great danger she hadn't gotten into of her own accord, and out of which nobody else could have helped her. Now someone had let her get back into danger of which she had no clear realization, and nobody else seemed to comprehend. Again nobody had any idea of how to get her out. This was not romance in any ordinary sense. But it was an infuriating thing to have happen. Trent clenched and unclenched his hands and fumed.

The news tapes all over the city—all over the planet, for that matter—murmured coyly of exciting news. The news was that the *Yarrow* had come into port, and the *Yarrow* was that gallant ship which had rammed a pirate and damaged it, so that Captain Trent could later recapture a ship that pirates had seized and bring it into port with pirate prisoners. The story was already being twisted and made inaccurate.

A spaceman who'd helped salvage the *Hecla* heard it. He'd gone out in the *Yarrow* to find the then-derelict ship. Now he was a hero, and slightly drunk, and he felt a fine sentimental regard for that old ship the *Yarrow* on which he'd gone out to accomplish fame. He resolved generously to visit his former shipmates and tell them of his triumphs. He began a not-too-accurate progress toward the ship. He encountered a fellow-hero of the *Hecla's* salvage. That friend knew of two more nearby. A newsman picked up the intended sentimental journey. He gathered the rest, and went along with his camera to get a picture and a story about heroes' friendships for each other and their plans for further anti-pirate activity. They wobbled a little as they walked, but their intentions were firmly emotional.

They got to the *Yarrow,* and the mate was tearing his hair. Word had somehow gotten out that the *Yarrow* was about to lift off. He was being besieged. A freight-broker, in particular, offered double freight and something extra for the mate to take one large crate to Loren. The mate did not know whether to pass up the business or accept it. The crewmen hadn't gotten back with the small arms and he didn't know what to do about it. Trent wasn't one to turn down business. He was called away to answer a message from the spaceport office. It was Trent, insisting on haste. A big truck ran the crate up to a cargo door. The members of the *Hecla's* salvage crew went into the *Yarrow's* forecastle for a sentimental greeting of their oldest friends. They weren't there. The salvage crew sat down to wait for them, and promptly fell asleep.

A totally frustrating and bewildering development infringed on Trent's plans. Orders from the highest authority on the planet commanded that no ship be lifted off or allowed to lift itself off from the spaceport until further orders. Police came and stood by, lounging, so that nothing could be done by the spaceport crew against these orders. More police appeared. Presently the spaceport was totally police-occupied. Trent protested furiously, and as he was a personage of some note since his capture of pirates, a high official told him in confidence that there'd been an ultra-long-range message from the other side of the solar system. It said that a ship bound for Manaos had been stopped by a pirate. Then it had been released, incredibly, but for the fact that it brought a message from the pirates. That ship was on the way and should land tonight. It had been in the hands of the pirates for two days while the message was prepared. The pirates then took half of its crew for captives and contemptuously let the rest go, to deliver their message. The remainder of the crew finished rewinding the overdrive coil. They'd come on to land at Manaos with the message. And they were being met at the spaceport by what was practically the government of Manaos. Because Trent had brought in pirates captured in the act of piracy, and they had threatened retaliation from their fellow-freebooters, and this message might be another threat.

Trent clenched and unclenched his hands. A message from the pirates might mean anything. It could even tell something about Marian. He found his throat gone dry. He waited. The news had come from a ship already broken out of overdrive. It was now driving at full Lawlor-drive speed toward Manaos, but it could not use overdrive in the areas where a planet had broken up into asteroids or where the elongated orbits of comets might interfere. But it would arrive before dawn.

And it did. It was a small and battered trading ship, and the landing-grid brought it down through lowering dark clouds that hid all the stars. It came slowly into the light cast upward from the spaceport, and it came down smoothly and touched the ground, and the large sleek ground-cars of officialdom went over to where it rested. Police blocked the approach of anybody else, including Trent. He found himself surrounded by newsmen and wondered bitterly how they knew what was going on.

The newsmen saw nothing. Trent saw no more. It seemed that aeons passed while the shiny cars stayed motionless about the landed small ship. It was far away over the spaceport tarmac, nearly as far as the lacy landing-grid reached.

At long last the sleek cars went away, escorted by police vehicles. Only one of them came toward the spaceport office, and newsmen broke the police cordon to get there first. Trent went along with the rest. This would be a news briefing.

It happened inside the spaceport office building, where

there was room for many passengers and their luggage to gather before they took ship and went away among the stars. Now a man with a disillusioned expression stood up on a table to make the official announcement of what was toward. His voice boomed.

"Some hours ago," he announced, "a message by microwave from the other side of the social system said that the ship *Castor* was coming in with a message from the Pleiad pirates, who had captured her, held her two days, and then released her minus half her crew. The message deals with the pirates taken prisoner and now held on Manaos awaiting trial."

Lights flashed at irregular intervals as the men with cameras took pictures to go on the morning news tapes. From time to time the harsh glow of longer-continuing lights for movie-tapes made the speaker look strange and unhuman. His face and figure were seemingly flattened by the excessive white glare. When more than one such light shone on him he shielded his eyes with his hands and gave them no usable picture. He went on loudly,

"The message was to this government and delivered in a sealed envelope. It announced that the pirates are now taking prisoners from ships they stop. They are, in fact, capturing ships to take prisoners. They swear that if their companions in our jail are hanged, they will hang—or worse—ten of their prisoners for each one of ours in prison here. The rest of the message tells of the arrangement by which we can communicate with them. The text of the main letter will be released later. The proposed arrangement for communication and for exchange of prisoners, of course, cannot be made public."

He got down from the table on which he'd stood to give the news release. Newsmen swarmed about him, barking questions they couldn't hope for him to answer unless he lost his temper at their insistence. But that wasn't likely. Police helped him to get his car through the senselessly jostling throng, with equally aimless flash-units continuing to make explosive white flames all about.

Trent went back to the *Yarrow*. Some time during the morning, he believed, he might be able to reach an official high-enough-up to get him an exception allowing the *Yarrow* to be lifted to space. After all, he had fought a pirate ship and won the fight in a limited degree. If any ship should be allowed to take to space, it should be the *Yarrow*. He could even—and here he knew a mirthless amusement—insist that he had to go out to space to try out McHinny's invention. It might work.

Actually, McHinny's gadget didn't have to be referred to. The *Yarrow* had applied for lift-off for the purpose of a voyage to Loren. Permission was granted, subject to carrying mail to that destination. There was no mention made of the huge crate containing an overdrive coil-unit to be delivered to a consignee there.

The permit and an extremely thin mail sack came to the ship by the same messenger. It may be that Trent should have put two and two together. He didn't, because he'd been trying to learn if the half-crew left in the small message-carrying ship had learned anything about a ship called the *Cytheria*. They hadn't. Therefore, Trent was savagely anxious to get to space. He didn't check on a number of things. The big crate. He didn't look in the forecastle.

It was just barely sunrise when the landing-grid's force field fumbled at the *Yarrow*, and tightened, and then began to lift the ship swiftly upward. It happened to be a very fine sunrise, with more different and more beautiful colorings than are often seen by early risers.

But the *Yarrow* went up and up, through the sunrise, to emptiness.

VI

WHEN THE SPACEPORT landing-grid let go of the *Yarrow*, she was a full five planetary diameters out from Manaos.

She'd lifted off at sunrise, spaceport time, and Manaos was a magnificent half-disk as seen from space. It was brilliantly green and blue where the sun shone on it and abysmally black where it was lighted only by the stars. But if one watched for a few minutes through a spaceport he could see the dark half of the disk displayed very faintly by starlight. With sharp eyes one could even see the ghostly specks and spirals of cloud-systems on Manaos' night side. Corresponding cloud-formations on the daylight side were blindingly white.

But Trent was in no mood to regard the wonders of the heavens. He aligned the *Yarrow*'s drive-axis for a certain fourth-magnitude star, the aiming-point for a ship intending a passage from Manaos to Loren. He snapped into the ship's speaker system, "Overdrive coming. Ten seconds. Count down."

He counted down himself, from ten to nine and eight and so on to zero. He pressed the overdrive-button and instantly fought dizziness and acute nausea and immediately afterwards that ghastly, spiralling, plummeting sensation as if falling through illimitable emptiness which goes with going into overdrive.

But then, abruptly, he was back in the pilot's chair, and the viewports were black as if sunk in tar, and somehow the normal minor operating sounds within the ship were consoling and welcome and deeply satisfying. Because they meant that the ship was alive and operating, and, therefore, it was going somewhere and, therefore, it would ultimately arrive.

Trent began to calculate in his head. While he'd been on Manaos, waiting for the *Yarrow*, no less than eleven ships had taken off for space in the bland conviction that because Trent had come out on top in a fight with a pirate, they also could now travel confidently to high profits before the rest of the Pleiads dared try it.

And the same thing had happened elsewhere. Ship owners on a dozen worlds, feverishly anxious for the profits they'd been missing, would convince themselves that the danger from piracy had diminished past the point where it needed to be considered. And most of those ships would make their voyages in safety because there were so many of them and a limited number of pirates could make only so many captures. But that didn't mean less danger. It only meant that the same danger was distributed among more ships.

Trent fumed about it, though it was strictly none of his business. Yet he couldn't help but consider it his business as regarded Marian. The ship she'd sailed on was statistically in less danger than the *Hecla* had been, but the improvement was in the probability of being captured, not the consequences. The disaster to any ship captured was as final as before. More, if the pirates were deliberately taking ships to get prisoners.

He couldn't sit quietly in the pilot's chair and envision such things. He got up and jerked a thumb for the man on control room watch to take over.

The man said, "Cap'n."

"What?"

"We got extra hands on board."

Trent stopped.

"Those fellows we carried out to the *Hecla*, sir. They come to say howdo to us. Pretty well lit, they were. We were over at the *Hecla* getting small arms when they come. They set down to wait for us. They passed out. They ain't waked up yet."

Trent frowned. He scowled. But after all, it made little or no difference. They might even come in handy.

"When they wake up, I'll put them to work," he said curtly.

There was nothing else to do about stowaways, especially these. Trent was not so concerned about rations or air that he considered them to matter. And they were trained in combat tactics. They made the *Yarrow* as heavily manned, but not armed, as any pirate ship would be. But this didn't happen to be an idea Trent found comforting. Marian Hale had gone to space for Loren. Just about now she'd be lifting off from Midway—if she'd arrived there—and would next be reported as landing on Loren—if she got there.

He went to the engine room. McHinny nodded porten-
tiously at him.

"I got my gadget built up again," he reported proudly,
"and it's better than it ever was before! It'll take care of any
pirate ship that ever was!"

"You're sure of it?" asked Trent.

"I know my gadget," said McHinny confidently. "Yes, sir!
Nobody's going to have to worry about pirates any more!"

Trent said, "It'll be too bad if we have to depend on it and
it doesn't work."

"I know what I'm doing!" insisted McHinny. "I know what
you're doing, too! You want to make it look like it's no
good! You handle it wrong on purpose! But you can't do that
any more! Not now!"

Trent grunted and turned to the engine room door. Mc-
Hinny said suspiciously, "I know what you think! You got an
extra overdrive unit in the hold because you think my gadget
might blow your overdrive next time you try to use it! You're
all set for it! But you wait! You see what happens!"

Trent went out. McHinny angered him, but it was good
to have something to be angry about which wasn't connected with Marian. He was in a state of acute, irritated
anxiety about her. He could make no plans for action, of
course. There was no proven need for it, and if it should be
needed he'd have no idea where to act, or how. He was
driving for Loren because he couldn't endure indefinite un-
certainty. If the *Cytheria* came into port on Loren with Marian aboard, he would be sure of her safety. He would also
have made a fool of himself, because he had no really valid
reason for going to Loren except to ease his mind. But if the
Cytheria didn't come into port with her aboard. . . .

It wouldn't be his fault. He'd told her he didn't think it
safe for her to put out to space. But it would be his fault
because it was his doing that merchantmen throughout the
Pleiads were taking to space under the delusion that danger
from pirates was now ended. And that had happened because he'd snatched her from deadly danger. Which he
couldn't be criticized for. But if he'd simply thrust his pirate

prisoners out an airlock the present situation wouldn't exist. So he blamed himself for not doing that.

The *Yarrow* had been in overdrive for eight ship-days and a little over when the alert signal went through the ship.

"Overdrive detector registers, sir," said the man on control room watch. *"Captain, sir! Our overdrive detector's registering!"*

Trent made his way quickly to the control room. There was a red light calling attention to the overdrive detector dial. There was another ship in detector-range, and it was in overdrive, too.

Trent took his seat at the control board. He gave crisp orders. All hands ready for spacesuits. Small arms to be passed out. He called McHinny and told him that his gadget might undergo an actual combat test. Then he watched, tensely, but somehow relieved that some sort of action might be substituted for mere frustrated waiting.

Some centuries earlier, a Captain Trent had lured a privateer out of a harbor where she was amply protected by the guns of a fort. He towed an improvised sea-anchor of canvas behind his ship. Because of the drag, his ship appeared both slow and unhandy. So the privateer came out to make a capture. In the forgotten fight that followed on one of Earth's oceans, at the proper critical moment Trent had the towline cut, and simultaneously uncovered guns of heavier weight and longer range than the privateer had suspected. He also revealed that the formerly logy and slow-sailing ship could not only out-fight but outrun the quasi-piratical ship that had attacked it. In consequence, the privateer's flag presently came fluttering down. And that Captain Trent put the privateer's crew into her boats with food and water, and he and his prize sailed away over the horizon while the left-behind privateers cursed him heartily.

But Captain Trent of the *Yarrow* could not look for such a happy termination of this affair. At the moment, the situation was simply a deflection of a needle from its proper place on an instrument-dial. He hadn't heavier guns than the other

ship. He had no guns at all. Further, he hadn't the legs of
the other ship. The *Yarrow* wasn't built for fighting or running away. And her overdrive unit hadn't the power per ton
of ship-and-cargo mass the piratical ship would be sure of.
In overdrive, the pirate ship could undoubtedly blow the
Yarrow's field-generating equipment without any trouble at
all.

But this was nevertheless action, after two hundred odd
hours of inactivity. Any kind of happening was welcome.

Trent watched the detector-dial. The other ship might
sheer off. If so, it was an honest merchantman experiencing
the jumping jitters because its detector would be giving a
positive reading too. If it didn't sheer off. . . .

It didn't. The strength of the signal picked up increased
steadily on the dial. The other ship was moving to close in
on the *Yarrow*. To all appearances, the prospects were for a
matter-of-fact approach to fatal nearness, despite such dodg-
ings and twistings as the *Yarrow* might attempt. The dial-
reading grew stronger still. Trent changed course. The reading continued to show a steady, closer approach of the invisible other vessel. It had changed course in pursuit. The
dial-needle neared that red band which meant a dangerous
proximity of two ships. When the needle touched the edge
of the red area, either one of two evenly matched overdrives
might blow out. But there was a black mark somewhere in
the red. If the needle reached that mark, the *Yarrow*'s drive
would blow. It would have to.

Trent spoke curtly into the microphone before him.

"Engine room," he snapped. "I'm going to charge your
gadget. Right?"

McHinny's voice, shrill and unreasonably pettish, snapped
back, *"Go ahead! Dammit, she's ready!"*

Trent had his finger on the charge-button which should
draw some thousands of kilowatts into the pirate-frustrator
capacitors, to be stored up and stored up until it could be
released in a surge of multi-megawatt violence lasting for the
forty-thousandth of a second. Nothing could withstand it.

Nothing! Any drive phased into it would blow with insensate violence.

He'd actually begun to put pressure on the charge-switch when he stopped. If the gadget worked, the other ship would be disabled. Its drive coil might be irreparably ruined, so its crew couldn't rewind it to serviceability. And it was not probable, but it was possible that the other ship might not be a pirate. It might be an honest trading ship with an inattentive hand on control room watch. Carelessness could happen.

He shifted his hand. He said into the all-ship microphones, "We'll break out of overdrive first. Get set. Three, two, one, zero!"

He flipped the breakout switch. There was dizziness and momentary nausea and the feeling of a horrible spinning fall. Then stars flashed into being out the viewports and on the vision-screens. The *Yarrow* made a curious bobbing motion, quaintly like a curtsey of greeting to the universe to which it had returned. There were stars by multiples of millions.

And there was a flaming yellow double sun to starboard, near enough for each of its monster components to have visible disks a third of a degree across. If a double sun could have a planetary system, the *Yarrow* would have broken out inside it. There was brilliant, glaring, intolerable light which was blistering until the viewports' automatic filters reduced it.

Trent said evenly, "I think we've got company. If that other ship goes on without stopping, its skipper ought to break the man in the control room for inattention to duty. If it doesn't go by. . . ."

The mate said stolidly, "You cut off the drive and the detector too, Cap'n."

Trent nodded.

"Either our overdrive or theirs had to blow some time soon. I cut ours to make it seem to blow. But if I kept the detector on, they'd know it didn't. I'm hoping. . . ."

He reached over and cut the Lawlor drive too. In or out of overdrive, the Lawlor drive propelled the *Yarrow* on her course. Where this encounter took place, of course, a Lawlor drive alone was just about as useful as a pair of oars.

"We're acting like a derelict, a crippled ship, anyhow. We'll see what the other ship does. Meanwhile I'll charge the gadget."

This time he did press the charge-button, to draw on the *Yarrow's* power-bank for thousands of kilowatts for minutes in succession, to be discharged at will in a practically instantaneous surge of pure electric energy.

There was a crash and a roaring which was a bellow. The smell of vaporized metal and distilled insulation ran through the ship. The crash was so loud that for seconds afterwards Trent heard nothing. The first sound his recovering ears did hear was McHinny's voice, shrilling profanity at the top of his lungs. Then he heard the air-apparatus running at emergency speed to clear away the stench.

He jerked his head at the mate. The mate vanished. Trent sat tensely at the control board, waiting. With increased return of hearing he noticed rustling, crackling noises which would be microwave radiation from the nearby double sun.

The mate's voice came over the loud-speaker. *"Captain, sir, the gadget's blown again. It just ain't any good!"*

Trent could hardly have become more tense, but it did seem that his muscles did tauten further. Yet the *Yarrow* was in no worse situation than it had been when it rescued the crew—and Marian—from the *Hecla*.

The cracklings and rustling sounds from the double sun were broken into. There was a specifically artificial sound from the space around the *Yarrow*. It was high-pitched to begin with, and it rose swiftly in pitch until it passed the shrillness of the highest of whistles. It was, of course, a single radar pulse, imitating in the Pleiads the sound-ranging cry of furry flying creatures called bats, on Earth.

"All hands," said Trent evenly. "Get into spacesuits and load all weapons. We've just been hit by a radar pulse. There'd be no reason for anybody but pirates to follow us out of over-drive and try to locate us by radar."

There were stirrings here and there. The mate came back and said, "Your spacesuit, Captain."

Trent got up from the control board and slipped into his space armor. There came another radar pulse. It was louder. For a long time after that there was something close to silence in the *Yarrow.* True, the air apparatus whirred and cut off. The temperature control made a new kind of noise. Now it was cutting down the heat-intake from the nearby double sun instead of holding the temperature of the *Yarrow* so many degrees Kelvin above the chill of empty space. And there were indefinite small sounds which came from the mere presence of living men inside the *Yarrow.*

There was a third radar pulse. The first had been like a squeaking. This was like a scream.

Then a vision-screen, turned away from the nearby suns, showed the blinkings of minute specks of varicolored lights which were stars. A voice came from the outside communicator, "*Privateer* Bear *of Loren calling. What ship's that?*"

Trent had, of course, anticipated the question. But he wanted to ask one of his own. Marian was off-planet somewhere in one of an unjustified number of suddenly foolhardy ships. All of them couldn't hope to escape capture by pirates. But the pirates couldn't hope to capture all of them, either. So the question Trent needed an answer to was, had the *Cytheria* been taken by this particular ship? If not, absolute recklessness was justified. The *Yarrow,* ramming, would not injure or endanger Marian in the process. On the other hand, if the *Cytheria* had been captured and Marian was one of other captives on this ship, then the maddest of recklessness was a necessity. Trent's most desperate obligation would be to smash the pirate at any cost because Marian was on board.

The ceiling loudspeaker bellowed, "*What ship's that? Answer or take what you get for it!*"

Trent growled, "This is the *Cytheria,* bound for Loren. And if you're the *Bear* you'll go about your business! You've blown our overdrive!"

Sweat stood out on his face as he waited to hear. If this

pirate ship had taken the *Cytheria*, they'd know the *Yarrow* wasn't the *Cytheria*. And they'd reveal it.

But the voice from outside the ship, from the pirate, was only almost mocking. "*It was the only way we could hail you. You tried to run away. What's your cargo?*"

Trent ran off a cargo list at random. It didn't matter. He didn't think of the huge crate loaded aboard the *Yarrow* on Manaos. He didn't think of it. The vision-screen showed a small glittering which now rapidly took on the shape of a ship. The voice from the ceiling speaker said genially, "*We can use some of that. We'll come aboard.*"

Trent's eyes burned, now. Marian wasn't aboard this ship. Therefore anything that could be done to deceive, to damage, or to destroy this pirate could be done from a simple, honest hatred of everything it stood for. And Marian wasn't involved. However, there seemed nothing to be done.

Trent protested as if angrily. The other ship took form as a polished fish-like shape. He argued feverishly, as if he believed he dealt with the privateer *Bear* of Loren, owned by the planetary president who happened to be Marian's father. Actually, it was conceivable that it was the *Bear*. Or the one that had attacked the *Hecla* was the *Bear*. But he didn't care. Marian was in danger, and therefore he didn't care whether it was a quasi-level privateer or an unquestionable freebooter. He meant to try to destroy it, legally or illegally, properly or otherwise.

Meanwhile he protested. His argument was that the *Yarrow*—which he called the *Cytheria*—was bound for Loren and the cargo she carried was to be delivered to that planet anyhow. As a privateer, insisted Trent, the *Bear* was bound to respect vessels bound for its home spaceport. It had done enough damage! It has blown out his overdrive. It. . . .

"*We'll give you receipts for what we take*," said the voice from the ceiling loudspeaker. It was almost openly mocking, now. "*You'll get what's coming to you. All you have to do is go on to Loren and ask for it.*"

Trent clicked off the communicator and swung about in the pilot's chair.

"On the way out to put us on board the *Hecla* when she was abandoned," he said coldly to the mate, "I had you pack the bow with bales of stuff in case a gun opened on you from ahead. None of that's been shifted, has it?"

"No sir," said the mate stolidly. "All of it's still there. You've got him sure our overdrive's blown, sir."

"And if we went into it," said Trent acidly, "he could really blow it just by following us!" He pushed the all-speaker button. "All hands! We've been stopped by something that says its the *Bear*, of Loren. It says we're to be boarded. All hands get ready to get out of sight and come out again on call."

He swung the *Yarrow* to face the approaching and enlarging other ship of space. He yearned fiercely to destroy it, but at that moment the *Yarrow*'s own prospects looked dim. For one thing, the first freebooter he'd encountered had a gun, a cannon firing solid shot. In a sense it was an antiquity. It was probably of a design from the twentieth century, when guns reached their highest development before being replaced by rocket-missiles. Its shells could penetrate both skins of the *Hecla* but had little power to do damage beyond that. One of the other pirate's shells had bounced around in the *Hecla*'s engine room without doing any particular harm. But those shells could let all the air out of a ship.

Perhaps this second pirate ship also had a gun. Against that twentieth-century weapon—outmoded as it was—Trent had prepared a nineteenth-century defense. There'd been a civil war in a nation called the United States, back on Earth, and in that war much action took place on the continental rivers. For this specialized fighting, river-steamers were converted into fighting ships by piled-up bales of a crude textile fabric then much in use. The river steamers became "cotton-clad" gunboats as contrasted with iron-clad ones and did good service. Trent had packed the bow of the *Yarrow* with similar materials. They should limit the penetration of solid shot fired from straight ahead.

The other ship was plainly visible now. It swiftly increased in size. There was no sign of injuries to or repairs of its bow portion, so it couldn't be the ship that had stopped the *Hecla*. It was larger, too. There were, then, at least two space craft operating out of some unknown base. There might be a number more.

The other ship swept to a position a mile to starboard. It checked there and lay still. The mussel-shell-shaped boat-blister covers opened, revealing spaceboats

Trent snapped into the all-ship speakers, "Men with rocket-launchers to the airports. Rope yourselves safe, and be ready to open the outer doors and start shooting."

He grimaced. He'd bought small arms on Dorade, but they'd been designed for police use. They'd be totally useless against a ship, of course. But they might do damage to a spaceboat.

He switched the communicator on again. The voice rasped, "*I'm telling you—open your cargo-doors! Open your airlocks! There's a boarding-party coming.*"

"Acknowledge," said Trent.

He covered the communicator microphone with his hand and gave short, savage commands. He opened an after cargo door. It stayed open. A second door started to open and apparently stuck. It went back to closed position. It partly opened and closed again. This could be seen from the pirate ship. It should be taken as attempted obedience. An airlock door opened. Another. The locks showed no spacesuited figures in them.

The pirate's spaceboats, three of them, moved away from their storage blisters. They came steadily toward the *Yarrow*. The two ships were infinitesimal specks in immensity. The spaceboats were smaller than specks. The blazing double sun alone was huge. It seemed nearby. All the rest of the galaxy appeared to consist only of uncountable dots of light of every imaginable color and degree of brightness, unthinkably remote. To someone with a taste for comparisons, this action was taking place in such isolation, such loneliness, such enormous nothingness that the isolation of a ship in overdrive seemed companionable by contrast.

The spaceboats were halfway to the *Yarrow*. Trent barked into the all-speaker microphone, "Close face-plates! Take ordered action!"

And he acted as he spoke. The *Yarrow* spun like a top to face the pirate ship and plunged toward it at maximum acceleration in Lawlor drive. But the motion seemed horribly deliberate. Lifetimes seemed to pass at intervals that were only heartbeats. The *Yarrow* rushed upon the pirate—but not quite exactly. She would ride down and destroy the nearest spaceboat first. The pirate did have a gun. It flashed, and there was that hundredth-of-a-second flaring out of smoke before the utter emptiness of space snatched it away to nothingness.

A shell hit the *Yarrow*. Its impact could be heard or felt all over the ship. Spacesuited men appeared suddenly in the open airlocks. Rockets—only police-rockets, but still rockets—streaked away from the open lockdoors. Four . . . eight . . . a dozen. One hit a spaceboat. There was a soundless flash. A shaped-charge satchel bomb went off inside the spaceboat. It had been meant for the destruction of the *Yarrow* should her crew resist the entrance of their murderers. But one spaceboat had ceased to exist. The *Yarrow*'s bow swung to bring a second spaceboat to close range for the rocket-launchers on the port side. The smoke-jetting rockets plunged. One of them exploded just the bare instant before another arrived at the very same spot. It was pure chance, but the spaceboat's back was broken, and other rockets hit, too. It was not possible to estimate the total damage from the *Yarrow*.

That elderly merchant ship continued to hurl itself toward the pirate. The pirate's gun flashed again. It was a hit. And again, a hit. And again. Every shell hit home. Every one went into her bows and vanished in the bales of textiles and crates of other cargo packed to serve as improvised armor plate.

In the control room the instrument board showed three bow compartments losing air. But the *Yarrow* gained speed every second. The pirate's gun flashed and flashed, and every powder-flash was followed by the crashing impact of a projectile. But the *Yarrow* could take this kind of gunfire for a while, anyhow.

The pirate couldn't take ramming. It went into overdrive while the charging *Yarrow* was still two hundred yards away. Trent drove his ship fiercely through the emptiness where the pirate ship had been. He swung around and headed vengefully for the third of the spaceboats the pirate had put into space. The *Yarrow* passed it at a hundred yards' distance and rockets flashed and streaked toward it, past it, and into it, but it seemed mostly into it. What was left did not look like a spaceboat any longer, and the *Yarrow* seemingly had all of space to itself.

The mate seemed pleased. He said relievedly, "I'll take some hands and plug those shell-holes, Captain?"

"Not much use," said Trent, coldly. "If we go into overdrive our coil will blow, unless the pirate goes slinking away. But as long as he's got his gun and shells he won't do that. We killed off a good lot of his men in those boats, though!"

The mate looked pained. "What'll we do then, Captain?"

"We'll have to try," said Trent sardonically, "to think of something."

But it didn't look promising. The pirate had a gun. The *Yarrow* hadn't. The pirate had an intact overdrive coil, permitting it to appear and disappear, to depart and return, and which would automatically blow out the *Yarrow*'s corresponding unit if Trent tried to make use of it. The pirate had lost a good half of its crew in the lifeboats. Perhaps two-thirds. It definitely would not go away and leave the *Yarrow* to its own devices. The only unusual thing the *Yarrow* had displayed was resolution and a furious willingness to fight. That amounted to a tactical surprise.

But the pirate was now recovered from it. It reappeared. With a raging deliberation, it lay off some two miles from the *Yarrow* and began to pound it with solid shot. When the *Yarrow* charged, the pirate went into overdrive again. The *Yarrow* could have followed, of course, but at the cost of blowing its coil before it had completed the conversion from normal space. It could only remain in the glaring, terrible unshielded sunshine of the double sun. When the pirate appeared, the *Yarrow* dashed at it. But the *Yarrow* had no weapon but itself that could do its enemy damage, and its defense was only partial, and even that, only when it was driving head-on for its antagonist. Sooner or later its bow-armor of cargo bales must fail it.

The sequence of a desperate charge while the pirate pounded it with its cannon, and the disappearance of the freebooter into overdrive, then its reappearance elsewhere to throw more solid shot became almost routine. Trent turned the *Yarrow* over to the mate and went to check damage. It is always interesting and sometimes useful to put oneself mentally in an enemy's position. He began to imagine vaguely what he'd be able to do with spaceboats if he used them otherwise than as the pirate had.

He began to count up possibilities. Spaceboats would be very poor targets for a gun firing solid shot. But they'd have to get to actual contact to be able to explode a shaped charge usefully. And if the pirate went into overdrive at such a moment it would take the boat with it. And the spaceboat might come back to normal space lightyears from any ship or planet or . . . anything. It would never be heard of or seen in all the centuries and millenia still to come.

Trent would have risked it, for himself. But the *Yarrow* and the men aboard it—

The engine room was still air filled. Trent went around to the tiny emergency lock intended to allow of passage to another of the ship's compartments even if one or more of them lost air.

He came out of the airlock in the cargo hold next astern. He saw the huge crate the freight-broker had practically dumped aboard while the mate was in a state of total confusion.

He looked at it. And if his many-times-great-grandfather, that Captain Trent of the Napoleonic period, or any one of his numerously-great-grandfathers could have seen the situation and followed Trent's reasoning, why, Captain Trent's ancestors would have been pleased.

VII

THE YARROW swarmed with activity as soon as he'd worked out what to do. It was the simplest imaginable solution to his problem as soon as it was seen. Only the *Yarrow*'s engineer was bitter about it. Twice he had attempted to use his gadget. Each time it had blown itself out with exhaustive thoroughness as soon as Trent tried to charge its capacitors. Now Trent had men hacking at the monster crate containing an overdrive unit intended to be delivered to Loren. Trent had had the sardonic idea that it was meant to be installed in a privateer intended to be the companion of the *Bear*. He disapproved. But now, suddenly, he had an idea that he could put it to better use.

A solid shot hit the *Yarrow*'s bow. There was the feel of a full-power Lawlor dash at the pirate ship. The *Yarrow*'s mate was not an imaginative person, but he could carry out orders he understood. The orders to be carried out just now were perfectly understandable. Gain time.

Parts of the shipped overdrive coil became exposed. Trent wielded an axe himself, to get the crate cleared away. The engineer, muttering bitterly, brought out cables from the engine room stores. With Trent watching sharply, he welded them to that perfection of contact needed when currents in the tens of thousands of amperes were to be carried. He led the cables forward to the engine room. With Trent checking every move, he connected the overdrive coil in the cargo hold to the overdrive coil in the engine room. He installed a cut-off switch.

The *Yarrow* now had two overdrive coils connected in

parallel. Each of them was designed to perform a very special feat, most simply if not lucidly expressed as making a hole in the cosmos around the ship, enclosing the ship in that hole, and then pulling the hole inside itself. With two such devices in parallel, when they were turned on together they should make a much larger hole than one alone. They should, together, have more power per ship-and-cargo ton of mass than the pirate ship could possibly have. If the pirate ship and the *Yarrow* were in overdrive at the same time and as near to each other as they were now, one overdrive coil would have to blow. Originally, it would have been the *Yarrow's*. Now it should be the pirate's.

Trent made his way back to the control room. The mate greeted him with relief.

"Another bow compartment's lost air, Captain," he said worriedly. "The old *Yarrow's* likely to get hurt before long. I've had a man for'rd checking, but it looks like if we rammed her now we'd get all smashed up—if we could ram her."

"We can," said Trent briefly.

He surveyed the situation. It appeared to be the same as before. The pirate ship winked into existence where nothing had been. It swung about, so its gun would bear on the *Yarrow*. The *Yarrow* rushed at it. The gun got three solid shot into the *Yarrow's* bow, and the pirate vanished into overdrive. There it was unreachable.

Trent said deliberately, "Overdrive coming. Three, two, one, zero."

The *Yarrow* vanished into overdrive.

The yellow double sun poured out its intolerable light and heat. As a double sun, it could not have planets or satellites of any other kind. There were no comets, no asteroids, no meteor streams. The only objects that could ever orbit it, even temporarily, were spaceships. Moments ago there had been two of them. Now, quite suddenly, there was only one. It came out of nowhere. For a long time it was quite alone. Then the other came out of nothingness.

This second ship now lay still, miles from the one that had broken out first. The second ship was damaged. There were shot-holes in its bow-plating. Some of them ran into one another. There was a deep dent where a shell had hit a hull-frame behind the plating and had not penetrated but had made a deep depression which spoiled the symmetry of its form.

It was, of course, the *Yarrow*. It had gone into overdrive immediately after the pirate ship. It had stayed there. The drive detector which told of another ship also in overdrive flickered and ceased to register anything. That meant, of course, that there was no other operating overdrive nearby. The pirate's drive had blown out. Now the *Yarrow* had come out of overdrive and could go back into it at pleasure. The pirate ship was in normal space and now could not leave it again. But it still had a gun. That weapon flamed furiously and solid shot moved through space toward the *Yarrow*. Trent shifted the *Yarrow*'s position. At this distance it would take many seconds for the despairing pirate's missiles to reach the place where the *Yarrow* had been.

They reached that place. The *Yarrow* had moved. They went on, forever.

"She blew," said Trent briefly, for all the ship to hear. "Now we might ram her, because she can't go into overdrive any longer. But we're all shot up. Better not."

A faint noise came from the loudspeaker overhead. It was a voice. It babbled. It screamed. It begged pathetically. It babbled again. It was a spacesuit in emptiness, and unintelligible cries came from it.

The mate said, "Somehow, Captain, I don't think those pirates would pick up one of us if we was floating out of a smashed spaceboat like this fella."

"No," agreed Trent dourly. "They wouldn't. But they wouldn't need to ask us any questions about where our home port was, or how many ships like us were working out of it. And they wouldn't want to ask us if we knew anything about a ship named the *Cytheria*."

So he tracked down the voice from a spacesuit that had been in a now-shattered spaceboat. The man in that spacesuit had found himself floating in absolute emptiness. In the confused, furious dashes of the *Yarrow* upon the pirate, both ships had moved many miles away from the spot where the spaceboat had been. Actually, the pirate ship was more than a hundred miles from the senselessly screaming voice. He couldn't pick it out with the naked eye against the background of all the stars there were. He was alone as no man can remain alone and stay sane. And his screamings had a specific cause. The man in the spacesuit could see the giant, double, yellow sun and feel its deadly heat. He screamed because he believed he looked at the two round doors which were the entrance gates to hell. And he felt that he was falling toward them.

The *Yarrow* picked him up, after an hour of searching, but nothing intelligible could be gotten out of him. He'd gone mad from terror.

The *Yarrow* arrived at Loren two shipdays later. She was landed by the spaceport landing-grid which rose half a mile from the wide flat plains of the colony world. Trent went aground and formidably to the spaceport office. His first question was about the *Cytheria*—if she'd arrived yet. She hadn't.

He said coldly, "Better tell your planetary president that his daughter's aboard her. You might tell him too, that his privateer has turned pirate, and he has reason to be worried. He and this whole planet may be in trouble because of it. And there's a pirate ship disabled but working hard to make repairs a couple of days' drive back toward Manaos. She's probably in unstable orbit around a double yellow star, but she may be able to patch herself up before the orbit breaks."

Then he said, "And I need repairs, too. But I'll do all right with some steel plates and some good welders. How do I arrange for that?"

There was agitation at the Loren spaceport, especially after the *Yarrow's* crewmen went aground and relaxed in the unprosperous dives outside the spaceport gates. The planet itself was not one of the outstanding human colonies in the Pleiads. It had originally been settled because of a genus of local fiber-producing plants which had a high luxury-value. For a time it prospered, producing fabulously soft and fabulously beautiful textile raw materials. The population went up into the millions, and there'd been a time when its spaceport was busy with ships from half the galaxy come to trade for *ghil* fiber. At that time a certain ecological difficulty seemed trivial. Earth-type vegetation did not thrive on Loren. The planet's native soil-bacteria were excellent for *ghil*-fiber plants, but not for potatoes or corn or commonplace crops like beans. To grow crops for human consumption, hormones and vitamin-base compounds and antibiotics had to be imported from off-planet.

Naturally humans, everywhere, have to carry the vegetation of Earth with them when they plant a colony, to supply the excessively complex food compounds the human race has adapted itself to require. Loren was highly prosperous for a long time. But it was a one-product world, subject to the disasters of a one-crop economy. And now it was a backwater world, its commerce stagnant and going steadily downhill.

Some of the people on Loren were excited about the *Yarrow*'s arrival because trade goods were scarce. Even a privateer which requisitioned cargoes and gave receipts for them—to be redeemed in *ghil* fiber on Loren—could not supply the imported items a population of five millions needed. So even a single shipload of assorted imports could make a wild flurry in the business world on Loren.

Some of Loren's inhabitants were disturbed because they'd felt that the planet was being boycotted on account of its privateer, and now learned that interstellar trade was practically destroyed by pirates and even a privateer must work only empty shiplanes to no avail. The *Yarrow* was actually the first off-planet ship to touch ground on Loren in four months.

A few of Loren's people felt a special uneasiness because of the disabled pirate ship of which Trent had made report. In modern times there were no such things as armies or navies, of course. Police officials had to take over many functions formerly handled by the military. Some of them came to Trent and asked searching questions about the conflict near the double sun.

"We made out," Trent told them, "because we'd packed bulk cargo in our bow sections and their shells couldn't do but so much damage. If you mean to go after her, you should be able to find her with radar, and you shouldn't have much trouble. She's short-handed. We arranged that. We smashed three lifeboats full of men coming to board us. Have your doctors been able to get anything out of that pirate we brought in?"

They hadn't. They were recording all his babblings and studying them painstakingly. There was no doubt about his having been a pirate. But since his present mental state had been produced by an intolerable emotional stress of horror and despair, his babblings were naturally of emotional matters only. From his incoherencies they'd deduced at least three pirate ships in operation and half a dozen ships captured, but they couldn't be identified. Nor could they get any clue to where his own ship was based, nor a description of that home world, nor anything else that amounted to useful information. He babbled and wept and pleaded not to be returned to space where great yellow suns were the gates of hell and drew him irresistibly toward them.

Trent produced data from Manaos. It consisted of photos and fingerprints and retinal patterns of twelve pirates captured by Trent in the *Hecla*. They were the men for whose execution—if it happened—other pirates had sworn to take revenge. Their capture had sent innumerable deluded ships to space again, and there could be no doubt of the capture of enough spacemen and space travelers to let the pirates carry out their most bloodthirsty menaces. Trent mentioned sourly that both Marian and the *Hecla*'s skipper said that pirate ship looked like the *Bear*, whose identity the pirate claimed while demanding surrender. Trent suggested that the police look up the spaceport records of the *Bear*'s crew.

They came back presently, intolerably distressed. The pirates waiting trial, or release, on Manaos had been members

77

of the privateer commissioned by Loren. What should they do?

"If it comes here," said Trent savagely, "blow hell out of it! But I rammed it. There are some repairs they'd have trouble explaining. It probably won't come. It'll go to its real base. It made use of you for information about space lanes and ship movements to make its piratical efforts easier. Now and then it brought in something. But you helped it to the best of your ability!"

The police officials went away again. They were embarrassed.

Trent supervised the beginning of repairs to the *Yarrow's* shot-punctured bow. They were not difficult. A few hull-plates had to be replaced entirely, but damaged frames could be straightened by equipment aground, and the shot-holes could be plugged or patch-welded and be practically as good as new. The inner-skin shot-holes required no more elaborate attention. The cargo bales damaged by shot came out. They were replaced by others. Loren's merchants offered to buy the damaged bales. They took them at a price to pay for the repair work twice over. Hopefully, they offered *ghil* fiber in payment, and Trent accepted it.

A ship went out to space from Loren. It also belonged to Marian's father. It carried a gun. Its bow was armored with sandbags inside. It carried guided missiles. It carried volunteers from the planetary police anxious to capture or destroy a pirate ship to make up for their embarrassment on discovering that they'd been an active partner of one.

The *Cytheria* did not come to port. According to the note from Marian, it had intended to leave the planet Sira the day the note was written. The letter had been brought to Trent, on Manaos, by the *Yarrow*. Immediately afterward, the threat from the pirates had arrived. Trent lifted the *Yarrow* from Manaos less than twelve hours later, when the *Cytheria* should just about have reached Midway. It should have left that planet almost immediately for Loren. It was certainly possible for it to have reached Loren even before the *Yarrow*.

It hadn't. It was now many days overdue.

The delay was entirely reasonable. The *Cytheria* could have gone to Midway by a roundabout route. It needn't have followed the regular ship lane from Sira to Midway. If there was a possibility of encountering pirates, it would be intelligent to follow a circuitous pathway. Pirates would tend to wait along the ship lanes with drive-detectors out and reporting the presence of any ship in overdrive for a completely unbelievable distance. If the *Cytheria*'s skipper had made the journey roundabout, it would mean a longer journey. The *Cytheria* might not be overdue, if one knew the courses she'd followed.

Again, there might be alarm on Midway—there had been when the *Yarrow* stopped there—and the *Cytheria* could have stayed in port to wait until the pirate danger genuinely abated. She might be peacefully aground. There might be no ground for worry. But yet again, there might.

Perfectly reasonable causes might have operated to delay the *Cytheria*. But on the other hand she might have been taken by a pirate. In which case, Trent couldn't know where it had happened or where Marian, as a captive, might have been taken.

Days went by, and more days, and still more. Trent reminded himself of all the separate reasons for the *Cytheria* to be delayed . . . roundabout traveling, very sensible. Alarms of piracy to make her stay in port—entirely reasonable, perfectly possible, almost convincing. But not quite.

Trent suddenly realized that he didn't believe any of them. He simply had no more hope that Marian would ever arrive at Loren in the *Cytheria*. He had no hope she'd ever arrive anywhere. He was simply, desolately, and arbitrarily convinced that the *Cytheria* had been taken by pirates. Possibly by the *Bear*, which certainly wasn't the freebooter he'd encountered near the double yellow sun.

He gave no outward sign of his conclusion. There was nothing to be done about it. True, the *Yarrow* was fit to take to space again. True, the planetary president had sent word, several times, that he'd like to speak to Trent. But patchweldings hardly mattered, and Trent didn't want to talk to Marian's father. He simply didn't want to. With piracy rife in the Pleiads, her father had let her travel. He was the owner of a privateer, and those who should know—Marian and the *Hecla*'s skipper—declared that the pirate of the *Hecla* affair not only claimed to be the *Bear* but looked exactly like it.

Word came that the planetary president was coming to visit the *Yarrow*, which had defeated a pirate ship near the double yellow star. He was concerned because the ship gone to dispose of that disabled marauder hadn't yet returned.

Trent said sourly to the *Yarrow*'s mate, "You can tell him that the police ship will have to rewind the pirate's drive even if it surrenders, if it's to bring that ship into port. Doing that will take time. You can say that maybe they had to use a guided missile on it and are trying to patch it up to come back. That'd take more time. Tell him anything you please. I don't want to talk to him!"

The mate asked, "What'll I tell him about the lady? His daughter?"

"Anything you like," growled Trent. "She should have written him what happened to the *Hecla*. But they say there's been no ship but us to land here in months. So they haven't had any off-planet mail unless in the one sack we brought here. Maybe he doesn't know about the *Hecla*. If he doesn't, you can tell him if you choose. I'm claiming salvage out of his pocket for getting her to port after she was abandoned. He'll probably dislike me for that. Anyway, I don't want to talk to him!"

"Where're you going?" asked the mate.

"Off somewhere until he leaves," said Trent. He shrugged. "I've agreed to take *ghil*-fiber for the money due us for what I've sold here. It's been suggested that I see what a *ghil* plantation is like. It was intended as a courtesy; I'll use it as an alibi."

The mate said nothing. Trent got a ground-car and left the spaceport before the planetary president could arrive. It was not polite, but Trent was past politeness now. The

Cytheria was at least eight days overdue by any calculation at all, if her skipper hadn't stayed aground on Midway. If she'd been captured by a pirate ship near the beginning of her voyage, she could have been taken twenty-two days ago, which was well before a battered small ship brought the threat of the pirate to Manaos. Marian could have been dead for three weeks. Or she might not be dead.

Trent drove furiously to the *ghil*-fiber plantation. He wasn't interested in plantations. It was unbearable to think of Marian dead or a prisoner of pirates who'd promised to murder ten spacemen or passengers for every one of their number hanged. It was time for him to take action. It happened to be impossible to take appropriate action, but he had to do something! So he resolved savagely to take to space himself as soon as the planetary president would have left the *Yarrow*.

He had no information, but he'd had a program in mind when he took command of his ship. The owners had offered him salvage rights. He'd used them, as the *Hecla* proved. He had the choice of ports-of-call and other privileges the owners had granted. He'd use them, though not as might be expected. He'd had some definite ideas about pirate-hunting, which should be an extremely profitable business if one didn't happen to be killed at it. He'd thought of it as an approach to salvage on a considerable scale. He'd preferred to have had definite information to start with, but since he was now suddenly and irrevocably convinced that Marian was dead, he'd set about hunting pirates anyhow, and somehow try to pay back whoever had harmed her.

Meanwhile, he drove to the *ghil* plantation to stay where Marian's father wouldn't be. As a visitor from off-planet who was actually buying *ghil* fiber, he was given red-carpet treatment at the plantation. He saw fields upon fields of *ghil* plants, and planting machinery and cultivating machinery and harvesting machinery. He saw processing equipment and a small research laboratory for improving the quality of *ghil* seeds. The laboratory was run by a squarish elderly scientist who took it for granted that anybody who saw a *ghil*-plant field would immediately be fascinated by experiments in line-bred mutant field crops. To the original purpose of his research he'd added a search for another plant than *ghil* to make a new one-crop economy for Loren.

He had tiny hot-houses in which he grew assorted samples of vegetation from more than thirty different worlds other than Loren. He maintained appropriate climatic conditions and growing-soil for each separate planet's vegetation in the separate plastic shelters. He almost—almost—aroused Trent's interest when he explained how he could describe the planet a plant came from by examination of a single plant or sometimes even a leaf. He could tell the composition of its atmosphere, its gravitational field-strength, the climate, its temperature range, and even its seasonal changes all from a leaf of an unidentified botanical specimen. Trent listened with what was almost interest.

But suddenly something made him turn away from this lecture to stare at the horizon behind him. The planet's landing-grid could be seen even from here, but there was a thread of white smoke uncoiling swiftly from within it. Something went blasting toward the sky. It reached the blue, went beyond. It thinned and thinned and thinned. Then it was gone.

And half an hour later a ground-car screeched to a stop at the *ghil* plantation. It had come for Trent. The *Yarrow's* mate had sent one of the crewmen to give Trent exact information. He was clearing away all scaffolding and getting ready to take to space immediately Trent arrived.

Because the *Cytheria* had come into port. An hour since she'd called down to ask coordinates for landing. The landing-grid operator had given them, and fumbled far, far out in emptiness until the grid's force-fields found and locked onto the ship. They brought her swiftly and precisely to ground. In the very center of the spaceport, the *Cytheria* stood upright. A man—one man only—came out of a passenger-port and trudged across the tarmac to the landing-grid's office. He went in and asked if there was mail for the *Cytheria*. There was. One letter. It looked official. It had come in the single bag of mail put on the *Yarrow* just before she was allowed to lift off of Manaos.

The single figure from the *Cytheria* trudged back to that ship, carrying the one letter in its official-seeming envelope. He went in the passenger-port. It closed behind him. The *Cytheria* asked by space-phone for immediate lift-off.

The grid office was astonished. This was so completely out of the ordinary run of events that the operator blankly asked why. What was the matter? Wasn't there any cargo? Weren't there any passengers to come ashore? Wasn't there one passenger in particular?

The operator should have focussed the grid's force-fields on the ship aground, as if perhaps to lift her. Then he should have held her aground in despite of protests or threats. He didn't happen to think of it. Such a thing had never been necessary or desirable. It was . . . unthinkable.

And the *Cytheria* suddenly emitted flames. They rolled over the empty spaceport tarmac. She lifted on her emergency-rockets and plunged skyward.

When Trent got to the spaceport, already three parts maddened by shock and frustration and grief, the *Cytheria* —which should have had Marian aboard to be landed here— was long gone away to space again. She'd long since gone into overdrive. She was already millions upon millions of miles away and traveling many times faster than the speed of light. And there was no faintest clue to her destination.

VIII

Things added up perfectly to a total of pure frustration. The *Cytheria* had been taken by pirates at some time which could have been anything up to twenty-two days before. At the time of her capture, the pirates knew that some of their companions were prisoners and were to be tried and doubtless executed on Manaos. Therefore she hadn't been looted and abandoned in emptiness. She'd been reserved for the task she'd just performed, of securing the official answer to their ultimatum. Her passengers and crew might or might not have been murdered at the time of her capture or any instant later. It was not possible to know.

These items fitted together. In making a demand for the exchange of captured pirates for captured spacemen and space travelers, the pirates must have named some way by which their demand could be answered. That hadn't been revealed on Manaos, but the *Yarrow* had been permitted to lift off for Loren with a flat mail sack before any other space craft was permitted to leave the planet. One thin, flat, official letter was probably the only postal matter in it. It was most likely the Manaos' government's answer to the threat.

Other things fitted in. If the *Bear* was both privateer and pirate, it would know the Loren spaceport and its personnel. It would know that the already-captured *Cytheria* could be sent there to pick up mail with no real danger of not being able to leave again. The fact that all interstellar communications traveled by ship made such an arrangement the only practical one. The other extraneous attempt to stop the *Yarrow* near the double yellow sun was simply proof that the pirates couldn't communicate with each other over vast distances. They got their supplies and information and delivered their loot—and now prisoners—at some base somewhere. Not all of them would be fully informed at any one time. The ship by the double star wasn't.

But the lack of any information about where that base might be—and a base was necessary—was frenziedly frustrating. Trent fiercely demanded information about the contacts of the *Bear*'s crew on Loren when as a privateer she happened to be in port. If the crewmen were recruited from the local population—

They weren't. The *Bear* had appeared off Loren two years before. Its skipper proposed a deal to the local authorities. The *Bear* offered to act as a privateer for Loren, artifically supplying the planet with off-planet goods. Loren would pay for them in *ghil* fiber on presentation of the receipts the *Bear* would give its victims. It would be a process for forcing the trade that Loren's economic crisis had driven away. To have even the color of lawfulness, of course, a privateer had to be owned on the planet it seized goods for. So Marian's father had formally purchased the *Bear*, but it was strictly a legal fiction. The *Bear's* skipper was her true owner. The *Bear* had brought in some cargoes. It got information and some supplies from Loren. But no man of its crew belonged there. There was nothing to be learned about their actual base from casual hints they'd dropped. They hadn't dropped any.

It was a dead-end query. It led nowhere. But nobody else on Loren had thought to ask even that. Trent surrendered Marian's letter to the authorities. It proved that she should have been aboard the *Cytheria*. The behavior of that ship proved that it had been captured, unquestionably while she was aboard. Her father became as horror-struck as Trent assured himself he wasn't. All the resources of Loren were immediately available for anything that could conceivably be done. And Trent became automatically the man to whom proposals were offered and suggestions made and questions presented.

He had questions of his own. He gave orders for a study of every bit of information about every planet within a light-century. The Galactic Directory wouldn't tell if there were one whose colonists had ceased to have normal space-communication with the rest of the Pleiads—the reason, pirates —or else one which could have had a pirate's base built on it. The second alternative was not too likely. Criminal enterprises are inherently destructive. A specially built base would be constructive. It would mean investment of capital, in fact, construction. The bare idea of building something would be alien to a piratical enterprise. It wouldn't be done.

The searching of records was a reasonable idea, but it was based on the assumption that pirates would maintain their ships in the manner of ship owners, keeping them in repair. But pirates wouldn't keep ships in repair. Instead, they'd abandon them for better-found ships as they captured them. So the urgent search of records was apparently futile.

But the news of such quests did bring one of the *Yarrow's* crewmen to Trent with an observation he'd made while the *Cytheria* was aground. He'd heard, naturally, of the search for a probably tiny colony whose landing-grid was at the service of pirates. He was one of the salvage-crew Trent had recruited for the *Hecla*. He'd been making a final weld on the *Yarrow's* bow-plates when the *Cytheria* touched ground. He'd seen lumps of frozen mud on the tips of her landing-fins. He came to Trent to report that wherever the *Cytheria* had been, it hadn't been to a Pleiad spaceport. He knew the Pleiad spaceports. They were solidly paved. The *Cytheria* had landed somewhere where there wasn't a landing-grid. She'd landed by rockets, ordinarily an emergency landing-system only. She'd taken off again. There was mud on her landing-fins. So there was no use looking for a known space-port that pirates might have seized.

Trent barked orders. He had no authority to give orders, but nobody else had orders to give. He was obeyed. He sent a ground-car burning up the highway to the *ghil* plantation he'd visited only hours earlier. The scientist there, with specimens of vegetation from thirty other planets growing in plastic cubicles was to be picked up and brought to him right away!

And Trent went out on the spaceport tarmac to see if by any possible chance any fragments of that mentioned mud had been left behind by the *Cytheria.*

He was, as it happened, just in time to keep tidy-minded spaceport employees from cleaning up and disposing of the left-behind mud as refuse.

It was nearly an hour before the white-haired scientist arrived from the *ghil* plantation research laboratory. Trent was pacing up and down, his hands clenching and unclenching, alternating between rage that he hadn't been at the spaceport when the *Cytheria* came in—she'd never have lifted off again without a fight—and bitter despair because all his most appalling suspicions seemed to have been proven true.

Meanwhile the lumps of soil from the *Cytheria*'s landing-fins melted. Exposed to a vacuum, water boils, and in boiling loses heat, so that when a certain portion of it has boiled away the remainder becomes ice. The first human-made artificial ice was made by the operation of a vacuum-pump on a flask of water. Wherever the *Cytheria* had landed before Loren, mud sticking to her fins had been carried away, frozen solid in space. It remained firmly fixed until the slight shock of landing on the Loren tarmac jolted it loose. The now-softened fragments amounted to a total of nearly a bushel of top-soil and plant-fragments.

The ground-car with the *ghil* plantation scientist arrived. Trent stood tensely by while he examined the material that so nearly had escaped being thrown away. The examination was exhaustive, done with pursed lips and an air of intense but academic interest. At long last he shook his head.

"I've plant samples from thirty worlds," he said regretfully, "but not from this one. Most interesting! This thready specimen is functionally a congener of grasses. It is a ground-cover plant. This one—I've never seen this leaf-shape or this triform stem before, and this—" He shook his head. "It looks like part of a symbiotic unit. Perhaps its companion-organism—"

"Where's it from?" demanded Trent.

"I haven't the least idea," said the scientist ruefully. "Not the least idea. But I hope I can take these specimens! They've been frozen, but possibly there may be spores or . . . or something that in a proper environment will revive and develop. They're most interesting!"

"We've got to know the planet they came from!" snapped Trent. "We've got to!"

The short man again shook his head.

"Nobody knows all the plants in the galaxy," he said in mild defensiveness. "Nobody! But of course—it's from a planet very nearly the size of this one. The stalks would be thinner on a lighter world, and thicker where the gravity was greater. The sun is type G, because of the exact variant of chlorophyl that has this special tint to use that kind of light. The cell-forms suggest a trace of sulphur dioxide in the atmosphere; not much, but a trace. And the soil says conclusively that there is much volcanic activity, because it contains volcanic ash in every stage of disintegration from fresh ash to, hmmm, sludge. But I bore you."

"Keep on!" said Trent.

"The temperature range," said the short man, "would be of the order of fifteen to forty-five degrees centigrade, which one knows by the evaporation-rates the leaf-surfaces imply. The planet's axis will be nearly at a right angle to the ecliptic, because there are practically no seasons, and I'd estimate the annual rainfall at about two meters per standard year." Then the ecologist said apologetically, "But that's all. I'm sorry I can't tell you anything really useful. But there simply isn't any information to tell what planet this material comes from."

"You're wrong," said Trent. "You have told me!"

Thirty minutes later the *Yarrow* lifted off to space from the Loren landing-grid. When it was well on its way, Trent painstakingly read in the Galactic Directory for this sector. He'd studied every planet within a light-century with no reason to guess at one rather than another, until the plant ecologist told him. He read:

. . . *mass approximately* 1/325000 *sol. Acceleration due to gravity,* 975 *cm.-sec. Solar const.* 1.94 *small cal. min. Mean bar. pres.* 794 *mm. mercury. Rotation period* 26.30 *hr. Atm.* 72.6% N, 27.5% O, .08% CO_2, .04% SO_2 . . .

The description in the Directory was of a planet not individually named, but known as Kress Three because it lay in the third orbit out from the sun called Kress. It was the only planet within a hundred lightyears whose physical constants matched the description given by the mud dropped from the *Cytheria's* fins. The *Yarrow* drove for it with all the speed two overdrive coils in one ship's hull could make possible.

It was related of one of the earlier known explorers, back on ancient Earth, that when he bound across what was then believed a boundless sea, he encouraged his frightened crew by discovering floating tree-branches in the ocean. They must have come from land, and could only have come from land ahead.

Captain Trent of the *Yarrow* had better information and a totally unlike purpose. But he was as much relieved when on the second day out from Loren the *Yarrow*'s drive-detector reported another ship in overdrive within detector-range. The other ship was ahead. Captain Trent cut down his speed, and overhauled the other space craft in a very leisurely fashion. He caught up to it, but at a discreet distance to one side. There was no question of blowing drives. The *Yarrow* went by, slowly, as if only very slightly faster than its unseen companion. The other ship neither sheered off nor closed in. Had it been a merchantman, it would probably have sheered off. A pirate might have closed in. Doing neither, and yet moving on the same course, each identified the other to its own satisfaction. Trent was confident that the other ship was the *Cytheria*, bound for the pirate's base of operations. Very probably the *Cytheria* identified the *Yarrow* as that pirate vessel presumably receiving the attentions of an armed ship from Loren, back by the double yellow sun.

The *Yarrow* went on. It passed the *Cytheria* and left it astern. In due time the *Cytheria*'s drive-whine ceased to register on the *Yarrow*'s detector. Trent had made no move against it, yet only a relatively short time ago he'd have abandoned all else and turned toward it. He'd have blown its drives and blasted a way into it with shaped charges if it hesitated to surrender, and he'd have gone raging through it like death itself. But that was when he believed Marian aboard it.

Now he was sure she wasn't. Because the *Cytheria* had landed somewhere between its capture and its call for mail on Loren. It would have landed to put off prisoners, most probably, and cargo, certainly, to have her light for her errand. With no cargo she was safe against stoppage by any burdened vessel. So Trent was confident that if Marian had been alive so long after the *Cytheria*'s capture she'd been landed on the world of the botanical specimens from her landing-fins. And in passing her as he'd done, Trent had gotten an exact bearing to her destination, which was his. But he wasn't through with her yet.

He knew the world to which the *Cytheria* should be bound. But he needed a guide to the exact spot, the precise location, the exact place among scores of millions of square miles of planetary surface to which pirate ships would resort. Finding a black grain on a sandy beach would be a promising project by comparison. But Trent left the *Cytheria* behind and went on to Kress Three.

McHinny came into the control room, humiliated and desperate. He wanted Trent's promise to try out his marvellous pirate-frustrating invention once more. During the waiting time on Loren he'd taken no part in the repair work. He'd labored frantically to rebuild his gadget yet again. It had been tried twice; and now it was rebuilt for a third test in combat. It couldn't be said that McHinny was resolved. He was frantic to force the acceptance of his genius. He was truculent and waspish and bitterly on the defensive, but he'd built the contrivance all over again. Now, he said defiantly, he'd found the weakness in his former design.

The trouble was that he hadn't allowed for a Lawlor drive in operation in the ship his device was to make helpless. When tested before the *Yarrow*'s owners, it was tested against a ship in overdrive, but not moving. It was lying in an overdrive field which kept it out of normal space. With a Lawlor drive operating in overdrive, the gadget blew itself out. But, with the new modification, it would blow out not only the pirate's overdrive, but the Lawlor drive too. The weak point was not only eliminated, the device became an infinitely better weapon against pirates.

It was not his nature to be humble or to ask a favor. He

was much more likely to be scornful and to demand. But this time he was nearly human. He asked almost tearfully for one more chance to prove his device, and hence his genius.

"All right," said Trent. He felt impatient. "If the opportunity offers, we'll try it again. But only if the opportunity offers! What we're about is too tricky to let us take any chance we can avoid."

McHinny couldn't refrain from a truculent statement. "You won't be taking any chances this time!"

Trent nodded. He was impatient. He was very, very busy. He had to keep himself from hoping on Marian's account. He had to remind himself that she was undoubtedly dead. He had to keep his mind furiously busy lest it begin to spin out reasons to hope. And what he had to do was not to be carried out by a man deceiving himself in any fashion. It had to be arranged and carried out in cold blood, with only one purpose, an utterly ruthless and merciless destruction of any man however remotely connected with pirate operations in the Pleiades.

It happened, though, that he was deceiving himself. In actual cold blood he wouldn't have felt the deep hatred and killing hunger that filled him. He wouldn't have experienced moments when his voice was thick with fury, though he denied it, and when his hands tended to clench and unclench of themselves as if lusting to do murder. But he was able to tell himself that this was not on Marian's account alone. This was righteous fury, normal hatred; the reaction of any honorable man to the fact that pirates made a business of murder for their strictly personal benefit.

And, whether in cold blood or hot, his brain worked well enough. He got the *Yarrow* into orbit around Kress Three without provoking any sign that she had been detected. He even found a hiding place for her in a peculiar, bumbling aggregation of mountain-sized boulders tumbling around the smoky planet in an orbit like a moon.

So far, everything was almost ludicrously simple.

The planet Kress Three was of typical third-planet size

among the solar systems of type G suns. It was a little smaller than Manaos, and a little larger than Sira, and very nearly the same as Loren. There were, naturally, only very slight differences in gravity among the four of them. Kress Three should have had ice-caps. It didn't. Its axis was parallel to the axis of its sun, and therefore normal to the ecliptic, and there would be no perceptible seasons such as summer or winter anywhere. Its atmosphere had a rather high CO_2 content, so the hot-house effect of carbon dioxide in trapping solar heat would operate. It would be warm. Also, there was a good trace of sulphur dioxide in its atmosphere. This meant that the seas would be acid, which modified everything. And there were volcanos.

Trent surveyed it with angry, questing eyes from the *Yarrow's* hiding-place among the mountains bumbling into each other in their orbit. Down below, on the planet, there were lines of volcanos, nowhere very far from a sea. There were areas where the ground was barely visible because of local smoke. There were coastlines, here and there, where steam bubbled up and swirled hugely in white clouds, some of them scores of miles in length.

But there were no highways, which can be seen from space much sooner than cities of ordinary size. There were places, to be sure, where vegetation flourished, but also there were vast fields of lava, not all of it cold, on which certainly no plants and perhaps no bacteria could live. Trent searched feverishly. The pirate's base could not be on a plain of un-cooled lava. It could hardly be where mountains smoked and poured molten rock down their sides. There were islands in the acid seas, but they were small and unlikely places for pirates to use.

The *Yarrow* floated among the huge boulders which dwarfed her. The planet revolved underneath her. Trent fidgeted bitterly. The radar-detectors insisted that there was no radar-scanning of the sky above the unpleasant, smoky planet. Trent hadn't expected it. Radars need to be watched conscientiously. In the pirate base they simply wouldn't be, if only because they couldn't be expected to report anything near a useless planet far from any normal, colonized world. Only passive devices like drive detectors, calling attention to their own reports, would be really useful. So Trent had taken up this position on normal, Lawlor drive, and so hadn't disturbed anybody. An overdrive would have been a different matter.

Evidence for it came before the planet had made one revolution under the *Yarrow's* hiding place in space. The space-phone speaker in the ceiling of the control room clicked, loudly, and then a voice said, *"What ship's that?"*

The *Yarrow's* mate jumped visibly. Trent nodded. He pointed to the space-phone cut-off. It was turned to "RECEIVE ONLY." The *Yarrow* could receive transmissions from other ships in normal space, but the microphone would not transmit. The receiver had picked up a voice from the ground below to a ship that must just have come out of overdrive.

"Who would it be?" demanded another voice sourly. *"We're coming in."*

A pause. The first voice again, *"Who's that talking?"*

The second voice, as sourly as before; *"Go to hell, will you? This is the* Cytheria. *Back from getting the mail on Loren. Where'm I landing?"*

"Same place you took off from. Any trouble?"

"Grid man started to ask questions. We lifted by rocket. Picked up another ship's drive on the way. You hear it?"

"No. Nothing," said the first voice. *"Shoot a flare."*

Trent took a deep breath. This was a break. He'd beaten the *Cytheria* here. She was going to land, of course, in normal space. There was no other solidity. And she was going to shoot a flare to allow of her location from the ground, so she could be talked down where there was no landing-grid, and yet a particular place of landing was requisite.

He saw the flare, a strictly emergency device when a ship couldn't be found by the grid-operator where it ought to be. This was a luridly red ball of flame, giving off millions of candlepower of crimson light. Trent got it centered on a vision-screen and turned up the magnification. He saw the

Cytheria, a glittering rounded form in emptiness. He heard the voices.

"*You're too far east.*" That would be galactic east, of course, not east on the planet now a gibbous disk beyond the *Cytheria*. "*That's better . . . A little more.*" Then, "*Good enough. We'll fine it when you get lower. Start down.*"

Trent watched the magnified image of the *Cytheria*. It was still tiny. It moved swiftly down toward the planet's surface. That would be the Lawlor drive helping to aim and control it on the way down, and making those fine adjustments a rocket designed for emergency use couldn't be expected to take.

Trent said over his shoulder to the mate, "Use a camera on the vision-screen. We're going to need pictures."

He watched tensely. There was a promontory jutting out into the sea. It was a good landmark. There were mountains inland. One of them smoked. The *Cytheria* went down and down, dwindling. The first voice he'd heard made curt comments from time to time. That voice was aground. The voice coming from the *Cytheria* replied. Profanely.

He heard the camera clicking. The mate was photographing the vision-screen with its pictures of an extremely tiny ship growing smaller and ever smaller as it descended.

Then there were heavy rocket fumes. White smoke. The *Cytheria*'s rockets were slowing her, now, to make a gentle landing. Up to this moment they had merely checked her descent. Now they had to stop it. The Lawlor drive became more important. It could neither take a ship off nor land one, but in cooperation with rockets the results were admirable.

It landed. Rocket fumes blew away. The space-phone said sardonically, "*Welcome to our city! Fancy seeing you here!*"

The voice which was the *Cytheria* swore wearily. There was a clicking in the space-phone speaker. Somewhere, a phone had been turned off.

Trent found fury shaking him. Then he said evenly, "I hope those pictures came out well. We're going to need them."

The mate pulled out the long strip of film. He peeled off

the paper strip of positive. He glanced at it and held it out to Trent.

"These will do," said Trent. "Get them printed as big as they'll stay sharp. They're our maps."

The mate disappeared. He looked dubious. But he would manage somehow to get the small, self-developed pictures reproduced. In the ordinary course of business, written records were normally photocopied as routine. The mate went to wrestle with the copier. Trent pressed the all-hands button, and his voice echoed through every compartment of the ship.

"All hands," he said icily. "I'm going aground. There'll be some fighting and some loot. Anybody who wants to be ship-keeper can stay aboard. He gets no fighting and no loot. Everybody who's looking for action get set. He does get fighting, and he does get loot."

He made no reference to nobler reasons for landing on a pirate-occupied planet where there would certainly be more pirates than the party the *Yarrow* could send to ground. He didn't speak of the possible rescue of prisoners whom the pirates would otherwise murder. In fact, he appealed only to the combative and the mercenary instincts of his spacemen. But that was immediately understandable. Actually, an exactly similar appeal by another ship captain might have produced no volunteers at all. But Trent had actually to choose two men to leave behind with the mate as ship-keepers. There'd be McHinny left aboard, too.

But for whatever reason, the crew of the *Hecla*, the salvage crew, and the crew of the *Yarrow* were ready to follow Trent anywhere. They'd been in action with him before, but their confidence in him didn't come from that. The real reason was that he'd led them in a stupendous brawl in the dives outside the Sira spaceport.

He listed the equipment he wanted each man to carry. Satchel-bombs, two per man. They were shaped-charge bombs, and they were highly dependable for demolition. There were detonator-bombs, used by police for the moral effect of their sound. Trent mentioned modifications that could be made to them so they'd have more effect, though they'd be less moral. It involved nuts and bolts and broken welding-rod and scrap-iron.

They'd also carry small-arms. Rifles, yes. Pistols, definitely. As the *Yarrow*'s crewmen envisioned themselves festooned with such an armament, an extraordinary atmosphere of cheer and enthusiasm developed. He ordered masks against their own fog-gas bombs, and he insisted that each man carry ample ammunition.

When they gathered, crowding, to get into the *Yarrow*'s spaceboats, the feel of things was curiously like a no-longer-remembered incident in the life of a Captain Trent of the late eighteenth century. That Captain Trent had taken three-quarters of his ship's crew in that ship's small boats, and rowed into a harbor with them in the murky blackness of a starless, moonless, abysmally dark night. That Captain Trent was leading a cutting-out expedition nobody else would have tried. He happened to succeed.

This Captain Trent pocketed folded maps, which were actually parts of the ground surface of the planet they were to land on. He got into the lead boat, having given instructions to all his followers.

The spaceboats headed down for the planet. Captain Trent's expression changed when they were well on their way. There was zestful, uniformed anticipation all around him. But in the blackness of the spaceboat Trent's face went bleak.

He was thinking, of course, that this foray was too late. If he'd been here upon this errand long enough ago, it could have accomplished something. Maybe. But now it was much too late.

Marian, he assured himself bitterly, was dead. She must be. He couldn't but be too late.

IX

THE SPACEBOATS landed within hundreds of yards of each other under a leaden sky. They'd made practically all their descent on the far side of the planet, where radar would not have spotted them, even were radar in use by this world's pirate population. It wasn't, but Trent wouldn't risk it being turned on for some accidental reason. Then they'd come in low and barely skimmed mountain tops with valleys in between sometimes filled with smoke. Finally they went down really low over the acid sea. Once, only hundreds of feet above the water, they passed a place where the circle of a volcano's crater rose only a little higher than the waves. It was like an atoll, with its lagoon hundreds of feet below sea-level and filled with surging lava instead of sea. From several places in the crater rim, sea-water cascades leaped down into the depression, and turned to steam before they struck.

The three spaceboats left it behind. Trent kept in touch with his followers by lightphone, invented by the inventor of the telephone itself. It was used mostly for ship-to-ship and ship-to-office communications in spaceports, where there was already enough interference. But it worked well enough here, except once when they were driving through a giant cloud of condensed steam blowing across the water from some submarine source of heat.

Trent let his small squadron down lower and lower when land appeared ahead. In the end they flashed across an almost circular harbor with an extremely narrow exit to the sea. There was vegetation here, sparse and with that starveling appearance of all living things desperately surviving against great odds.

The spaceboats landed, kicking up clouds of volcanic ash. Trent's followers disembarked. The air smelled strongly of sulphur-fumes. Where there was volcanic activity on such a scale, there would be sulfur in every breath a man drew. One man sneezed. Another, and another.

"Use your masks," commanded Trent. "They'll take care of matters for a while. We'll probably get used to it. Now, look here!"

He spread out the enlarged copies the mate had made of the pictured descent of the *Cytheria*. The landing party crowded around to see. They were an extraordinary group to look at. Most of them would have made an ordinary citizen uneasy if he'd encountered them in some dark alley. There were tall men and short ones, and bulky ones and spare ones. But each had the indefinable air of men accustomed to take care of themselves. And they had a comfortable confidence in Trent.

Trent traced out items on the space photos.

"Here's the *Cytheria*," he observed, "heading down to this spot. It's a sort of a pothole of a valley with mountains almost all around it. Here and here you'll see things that look like spires of stone. They aren't. They're ships."

Men crowded closer, staring over each other's shoulders to see the pointed-out objects.

"I've counted," said Trent, "and there are thirty-odd of them, counting the *Cytheria*. She landed by rocket with her Lawlor drive to help, of course. In this photo she's not yet aground. In this one she is. Here's the blast-area her rockets burned away when she hovered to land gently. See?"

There were murmurings of assent. Trent's crewmen took turns looking closely. They appeared much more piratical than pirates would. Every man had two shaped-charge satchel bombs, dangling from his hips, and there were grenades in their belts and bandoliers of cartridges across their shoulders. Every man had automatic pistols and a rifle.

"The point," said Trent, "is that where she landed her rockets burned away what green stuff there was. There are seven other ships—they look like pointed rocks—with burnt-away places around them. There's no burnt area around the rest. You see what that means?"

They waited to hear. It was not that they couldn't think,

but they were content to let him do their thinking for them. A man sneezed. He'd taken off his gas-mask. He put it back on.

"When a ship's landed on rockets," Trent pointed out, "it stands in a scorched place. If it doesn't take off again, after a while the green stuff grows back. There are twenty odd of them with the green stuff returned. They've been aground a long time, some of them maybe years."

A burly man grunted. He had a scar on his cheek.

"They brought 'em here after they captured 'em," he said confidently. "They looted 'em as they felt like it. Then they left 'em where they were."

Trent nodded.

"Which means," he explained, "that we aren't up against the crews of thirty pirate ships. Those twenty-odd ships are carcasses, brought here to be rifled and then left to rust. And not all the lately landed ships are pirates, either. Some of them were brought in lately to be stripped. We may be up against odds of two or even three to one, but not more. And we'll have surprise on our side. We shouldn't have too much trouble."

Grins went around the group. Nobody spoke, which was a good sign. Nobody needed to assure himself of his own courage.

"Now, here's our route," said Trent. "Like this."

He traced it out. He'd picked it out carefully. It could be followed easily enough by day, of course, but for night guidance he'd mentally marked down where for a mile or two they'd trudge along the seashore, and farther where an active volcano should throw a glow against the sky, and another place—

We want to hit them just before sunrise," said Trent. "We'll be able to take a rest, I think, just this side of where we'll find them. So . . . let's go!"

In minutes he was leading his file of nearly thirty men away from the landing place. The spaceboats were partly covered by the ash in which they'd landed. Judging direction by the landmarks he noted, and thereby establishing a bearing for the sun, he headed toward the planet's south. He was, of course, as much burdened and as well-armed as any of his men. He led them across a rocky ridge and down on the other side again. There he found a patch of flowers. They were, as it later developed, the only blooms he was to see on the third planet out from Kress. They were utterly white, and very large, and somehow they looked artificial. They made one think of death.

The skies were somehow smoky, and the sun seemed redder than when seen from space. The air had the smell of sulphur, of which a very, very minute quantity seemed able to get through the gas masks, but in time they seemed to become used to it. After the first hour or two it became rare for anyone to wear his mask more than half the time. But the sulfur smell was annoying. It came from the volcanos, of course.

They tramped, and rested, and tramped again. There were places where spindling, somehow skeleton-like trees with white bark and extravagantly spreading branches struggled to attain a height of seven or eight feet. There were other places where thready green plants—but the green was not quite of vegetation brought from Earth—covered the ground so that men's boots crushed them and left clear trails where the plants had been.

They saw no animals. It was not to be doubted that animals existed, of course. Trent himself more than once saw tiny movements out of the corner of his eyes, but he didn't actually glimpse anything to be called an animal. Near sundown, though, they waded through a small brook—Trent tasted its water and it had a bare taste of rotten eggs in it, but it was drinkable—and they saw things that would probably be considered fish. And a mile or so farther on a small thing with many legs ran away from them with a clattering sound. It was more like a crab than any other familiar creature, but one doesn't usually think of a crab as an animal.

When the sun set in smoky redness, they were marching beside an oily, sulfur-scented sea. The beach was volcanic ash. There were giant mountains far away which poured out thick smoke and formed inky clouds which were blots against the sunset sky.

Night fell, and the smell of the sea made all of them keep their masks on for a great deal of the time. Those who didn't, sneezed. Trent turned on the space-phone he'd removed from a suit of space armor. He listened. If there were any communications going on, he'd hear it. He could have heard if the *Yarrow*'s mate tried to reach him from the ship. But he heard no voices nor any other sound in the space-phones.

There were things to hear when he took off the ear pieces, though. Noises that he'd become accustomed to were suddenly loud and distinct. The landing party was resting where they were, a thousand feet above the sea, when there came a deep, deep bass rumbling underground. Now, paying close heed to such things, Trent could detect occasional tremors in the rock he rested on. And suddenly he heard a strange, rumbling sound to seaward. It came nearer. It became a bellow and then a roaring and a more-than-thunderous shout.

The sea rose below them. A volcanic tidal wave hurled itself against the shoreline. The noise was ear-shattering. It meant utterly irresistible power and thousands of millions of tons of sulfur-smelling seawater flinging itself against the land.

It subsided. For a long, long time there were trickling, pouring, washing sounds from the rocks between the landing party and the sea. The water the tidal wave had flung upon the land was running back. The smell of the ocean was overpowering. If Trent and his followers had been in the way of that monstrous ocean movement, they'd not be alive now.

"There's always something going on, isn't there?" said Trent in a dry voice. "We might as well carry on."

He led the landing party on through the night. They marched, and they stumbled, and now and again Trent looked at his watch. Then they rested for ten minutes. They saw glowings in the sky, and the ground rumbled underfoot, and now and then there were perceptible tremors. And time passed, and the stars moved westward in the smoky sky. But miles passed, too. And at long, long last they went down a ravine. They'd been so long in the darkness that starlight was now enough for them to pick their way by.

The pirate rendezvous had been inspiredly chosen. There were mountains on nearly every hand, but these seemed not to be volcanos. Their edge against the stars spoke of an upheaval so gigantic that instead of a mountain, a mountain range resulted. The pirate's ships stood in a remarkably flat valley-bottom between rows of peaks. There was a partial gap to the southward, though, and very many miles away something seemed to explode. The sound of a racking detonation arrived, turned to deepest bass by the distance. The ground shook, and then a flame appeared. But instead of rising it flowed downward. It was incandescent lava pouring down a distant mountain flank. Even so many miles away, it cast a faint light into the valley, and the silent, upright ships of space were outlined by it.

Trent said very quietly,

"I showed you the ships you're to work on. You can be certain in the dark by feeling the ground. If there's something on the order of grass underfoot, that's wrong. The ones you want have only ashes under them. Get set. I'll give you time. When my first bomb goes off, go ahead!"

He moved away in the dimmest of possible starshine with a single companion, the burly man with the scarred cheek. His other followers separated. Then for a long, long time there were no noises that could be attributed to them. The far-away mountain exploded again. White-hot rocks rose above its top, fire-bombs flung skyward by the titanic forces at work yonder. There were flickerings of light where the pirate ships stood upright. The intermittant glare of the eruption reached so far.

Trent and the scar-faced man went quietly through the night. It was not likely that the tumult in the distance was unusual. This world was in a state of vulcanism such as seems always to occur on third-orbit planets of type G suns, just as all such worlds are denser for their size than their sister-planets. The pirates who'd chosen this spot for their base must have accumulated the looted ships during a considerable period of time. They'd be familiar with such phenomena as went on now. Those who were asleep would hardly stir. There would not be many awake an hour before sunrise. Discipline would be of the slackest among pirates, anyhow. Secure in their hiding-place, they couldn't be made to keep a conscientious watch except against their prisoners. And the captives would most likely have been put into a looted ship whose locks and cargo doors could be welded shut. Imprisoned so, they could find their own food, and attend to their own necessities, and if they happened to run out of food and water in those hulks, there was neither any way to ask nor any hope in asking for food from the pirates.

Trent found a ship with only ashes around its bottom. He and the burly man conferred in whispers. Trent set a satchel bomb in place. When it went off it should blow one of the ship's three landing-fins to scrap-metal. The ship could not stay upright on two supports. It would topple. And then they could take further action. The explosion of the first bomb would be the signal for the rest of his spacemen to begin their work. It had not been pictured to them as high or noble adventure and they wouldn't act that way. They'd make no dramatic gestures. But they would feel a fine zest, some part of which would come of acting as a team under a leader like Trent. This was quite independent of any prospects of profit. They followed Trent. It was even more satisfying than that brawl outside the spaceport on Sira.

There were many stars shining in a smoky sky. There were distant, muted explosions on a diminished scale. Trent set the timer on the satchel bomb. He and his companion drew off.

Seconds passed. The satchel bomb went off. Its shaped charge flashed blue-white and made a detonation sound so sharp and savage that it was like a blow on the chest. Then, very sedately and with a certain enormous leisureliness, the hull of this spaceship leaned. The first second it leaned only a little. But it gathered speed as it fell.

Before it had fallen a quarter of the way, other blue-white flashes began. Like super-super photographer's strobe-lights, they illuminated all the valley and the mountainsides about it. It would have been an impressive sight had the flashes been continuous. Twelve spaceships, pointing toward the sky, formed an indefinite group. Seven of them leaned and fell. They struck each other. They struck still-upright other ships. They crumpled, or they bent, or they went down in straightforward crashes that made the ground jump when they landed. And all this happened in the fraction of a minute.

There was a curious stillness for a moment. The lesser explosions of the mountain to southward increased. They became practically continuous. They sounded like a faraway cannonade, but no man in this generation had ever heard a cannonade save in recordings of ancient warfare. The fallen ships made strange small squeakings as vibrations of the ground helped them to settle in more stable relationships to each other.

Somebody bawled, *"Cap'n! Cap'n Trent!"*

Trent did not answer. He made his way toward the voice. Twice, as he went past fallen ships, and once under a vast cylinder which had fallen across another, he heard batterings. Men had been wakened by the falling of their ships. Those who did not die then hysterically tried to escape. But there were many who were actually trapped. A good and considerable number had been killed. And whatever might happen to Trent and his landing party, these strained, twisted, racked and not infrequently torn-open ships could never be taken to space again by the pirates who'd brought them here. For one thing, they'd have to be raised to vertical positions. Equipment for that purpose couldn't be improvised.

The voice bawled again, *"Cap'n! Cap'n Trent!"*

It was very near. Trent said, "What's the trouble?"

"Cap'n," said the voice anxiously, "we knocked down a ship, and it kind of split open, and there's a woman in it!"

Then a grenade went off a little distance away. A rifle cracked. A man screamed. There were other sounds of combat.

From a distance great enough to let all the grounded

ships be seen at once, there would have appeared to be very little activity of any sort. There were the occasional cracklings of firearms. They made tiny sparks. Now and again—rarely, now—there were explosions of other sorts. They made flashes. Sometimes they were satchel bombs. More often they were grenades.

Trent said shakily, "Marian! You're all right? The others—"

Marian said in a queer voice, as if she still couldn't believe in what had happened, "They put us . . . hostages in that ship and welded up the ports. They'd ruined the engines and the drive. They told us if the *Cytheria* didn't bring back . . . agreement to their terms they'd . . . bring us out and . . . make pictures of . . . of what happened to us . . . before we died. And they'd send those tapes with word that they'd take more prisoners and . . . do the same unless—"

Trent's throat was dry and seemed to be trying to shut to strangle him. At the same time his voice was thick and furry with hatred.

"I said are you all right? All of you?"

"We're quite all right," said Marian unsteadily, "only we . . . don't quite believe it."

There were eight or ten women and three men released from a welded-shut ship-hull by its fall. Strangely enough, as prisoners waiting to be the victims of carefully photographed atrocity, they had been made afraid by the recurrent minor shocks and tremors of this valley. Instead of staying in the cabins and accommodations of the ship's bow, they'd huddled in its sternmost part, nearest to the ground. The bow of a ship would be hundreds of feet high and it could have a completely destructive fall. But the stern section could only overturn. This ship had been toppled because it was lately landed and the ground was scorched beneath it. The prisoners in it, being merely shaken up by their trivial fall, had crawled out of a lock door twisted open despite its welding. They'd come out expecting to be recaptured or murdered. They'd had no hope to urge them; only fear. But Trent's men were not inclined to kill women. They'd bawled for him when the freed prisoners were discovered.

"Stay here," he commanded fiercely. "Guard them until we clean up the mess!"

He went away again. There was still darkness everywhere, but to the east an infinitely faint, rosy fading of the sky began. A rifle on automatic fire spat spiteful sparks to the left. Trent went to it. A grenade exploded farther on.

"What's going on?" he demanded. He was filled with remarkable emotions. Marian was again out of a predicament in which the folly of other men had involved her. He and he alone had proved capable of action to get her out. He was succeeding. "What's going on?" he demanded almost genially.

A member of the *Yarrow's* crew spat with great deliberation.

"Some characters in this ship here are tryin' to get out. Three-four got out. We bagged 'em. Now the others are hollerin' crazy-like. They want to know who's shooting."

"Tell them Santa Claus," said Trent. "Why not a grenade?"

He moved away. He heard the grenade explode behind him. Something huge loomed before him and overhead. It was the nose of a fallen ship. He heard sounds from inside it. Its control room viewports, or some of them, had been smashed in its fall. Now a loud speaker incredibly gave out speech from inside there. A savage, half-hysterical voice raged; *"Somehow somebody's landed here! Get to the Jocunda! Fight your way here and make it fast!"*

Somewhere in the valley an occupied pirate ship hadn't toppled. Somewhere a freebooter remained upright, and in some manner it had become aware that the noises outside it were not distant detonations but nearby bombs. It called to what other ships contained their crews. To a great degree that call was bound to be futile. But Trent found a specific object for his hatred. This ship would be in a sense the headquarters ship of the pirates of the Pleiads. It remained aground; it had stayed aground so long that green stuff grew about its base. It would have been kept provided with fuel and air-stores, ready to be used for escape should such a thing unthinkably be needed. Now it called on all pirates not trapped or disabled to join it. Most of them wouldn't hear it. Space-phone units would mostly have been shattered by the long fall of the fated ships' bows. Of those who survived, such as Trent had heard, most would be found in crushed and empty control rooms. Men in a ship that had fallen crashing from the vertical would either be dead, or they'd be injured, or they'd be trying frantically to get out to the sulfur-smelling out-of-doors.

But there were some who'd probably gotten their warning before Trent overheard the message. If he'd kept his personal space-phone turned on, he'd have known. More, the *Yarrow's* mate, aloft with those gigantic boulders which should have been a moon, would have heard the hysterical command. He'd be worried, but at least he'd know that the landing party was aground and was in action against the pirates.

The redness to the east grew brighter. Trent saw a man running crazily. He was not armed as the members of the landing party were. He was in flight. He passed behind a hulk that half an hour earlier had been a spaceship at least capable of lifting to the sky. He came out, running toward a group of still and silent ships standing on green-covered ground. Somewhere a rifle racketed in automatic fire. The running man collapsed. Trent growled. He headed in that direction.

Another man. Two others. They'd been warned by space-phone, but they didn't attempt to fight. They ran like deer toward the spires which were landed and looted and rusted space craft. A rifle cracked on one-shot fire. It cracked again, and again. One man fell all of a heap, his arms flailing. The solitary rifle began again.

Trent couldn't stop it, so he stood still, straining his eyes in the slowly, slowly increasing crimson light to see which of the presumable hulks they fled toward. That one mustn't lift off. It mustn't!

A running man fell. More than one rifle concentrated on the last man afoot. They made popping sounds. He began to zigzag crazily. He knew that the bullets whining past were aimed at him. He must have known that several men were shooting in the zestful competition of a sporting event.

He fell, and rolled over and over, and lay still. But Trent had identified the supposed hulk which had been his hope of refuge. He began to gather men for an assault upon it. There was a woeful lack of satchel bombs. Most of them had been used to admirable effect. He started toward the group of abandoned ships, of which one must be called the *Jocunda* and contained at least some of the pirates who a half-hour since had snored in their sins while Trent and his men came down into the valley.

There were flames. Monstrous flames spurted out from beneath a rusting hull. That would be the *Jocunda*. She rose from the ground, spouting hellfire. The flames were blue-white and so intense that for long moments the increasing ruddy light of dawn seemed whitened. With its Lawlor drive giving all possible help to its rockets, it crawled, then climbed, then seemed to fall toward the smoky heavens overhead. Trent watched it bitterly as it dwindled to a speck which in the red light of sunrise looked like a ruby in the sky.

Then he switched on his space-phone. He began to call, "Calling *Yarrow!* Calling *Yarrow!* Trent calling *Yarrow!*"

Almost instantly the mate's voice came back. It sounded relieved.

"Come in, Captain! I've been hearing some fancy stuff from aground there. You all right?"

"Yes. Some mopping up, but, is McHinny's gadget set for use?"

"Yes, sir. All set."

"There's a ship coming up," said Trent. "It got away. Tell him to try his gadget on it. He claims it'll work on a Lawlor drive, too, now. If it doesn't, use our two coils to blow their overdrive."

"Yes, sir! Anything else?"

"Nothing," said Trent.

Now, and it seemed very suddenly, the sun rose in splendor, with the sky a vivid crimson until past the zenith. All the mountain flanks glowed a ruddy color, and the valley of the pirate base was filled with multiple reflections of the rosy glare.

Again there seemed little activity of any sort. But Trent walked leisurely back to what activity there was. He picked up half a dozen men. He led them into a toppled ship. He and they made full use of their training and their rehearsals of combat tactics in the recesses and corridors and the corners of the less-visited parts of a spaceship. When they came out—they'd entered by a cargo door, but they came out through an airlock—they brought three injured men and they left others behind who would need burial later.

They went into a second ship. There were two shots from inside this one. A third. Trent was satisfied with the quality of their behavior. In his presence they felt some embarrassment about looting. He left them and put a second group of six to work on other ships.

Presently he came back to Marian. She looked tensely composed, but her eyes brightened when she saw him. She took off a space helmet a *Hecla*-salvage man had brought out of a ship. The former prisoners were all supplied and the man of the *Hecla* salvage operation looked at once complacent because of their gratitude and gloomy because he'd missed his full share of the fighting.

"I think," said Trent, "that we're doing all right. Do you know of any other prisoners?"

"We . . . were told there were some," said Marian. "They're welded in one of those hulks. They're waiting as we were . . . to be killed if the *Cytheria* didn't bring back acceptance of the pirates' terms."

Trent nodded to his followers.

"Take a torch, if you can find one," he ordered, "and look over those ships. Any that are welded shut, cut open and let the people out: Of course there may be one or two pirates left. Use your own judgement."

The group of *Yarrow* and *Hecla*-salvage hands went briskly and hopefully away. They would find prisoners in not less than three of the twenty-some still-standing ships. They'd be unaware of what had happened in the valley since just before sunrise. They'd be terrified when called on, believing it a summons to atrocity and murder. And they would be hysterically grateful when they found out it was not.

Then the space-phone dangling from Trent's neck made noises.

"Calling Captain Trent! Calling Captain Trent! Yarrow calling Captain Trent!"

Trent answered, and the mate's voice sounded exultant to a degree Trent had never heard before.

"The gadget worked, Captain! It worked! McHinny worked it himself, with the rising ship in plain view and rising right past us. She cut her rockets and flicked into overdrive and we hit the overdrive button with McHinny at the gadget in the fraction of a second afterward! And she popped back out to normal space! She's still rising, but she can't accelerate any more! Her drive and her overdrive are both blown out and she's losing velocity! She'll go up a while longer, and then she'll fall back! I figure she'll hit somewhere in mid-ocean in two hours and a half. But she'll be half-way melted down when she hits, and what's left will never come up again!"

"I don't suppose it will," agreed Trent. "All right. Very nice work! I'll call you back later."

He turned to Marian. She looked at him with warm eyes. He said, "There's a lot of stuff to attend to. We have to make sure about mopping up any pirates who may still be loose. I don't think there'll be many. Then we have to get the prisoners organized, taking care of their own food and so on. There are more than a hundred of them. And we have to find out if any pirate ship is still out cruising. I don't think there will be, but the *Yarrow* can blow the drive of any other ship in space, with two overdrive coils in parallel. We don't have to worry about them!"

It was not exactly the sort of speech a man would be expected to make under the circumstances. It was very businesslike. In fact, he was talking business.

"Then," he said, frowning thoughtfully, "I have to post salvage-claim notices on the ships here. I have to make a formal claim that each one has been made available for recovery and repair by my actions, in my chartered ship—I've salvage rights—and my men in my employ. Actually, I can sell these ships where they are, the purchasers to come and repair and remove them. I may do so if I need funds. But most of them will be salvaged like the *Hecla* was, and I'll claim salvage on each as I did on the *Hecla*."

She listened. But her expression became uncertain. It was even puzzled. She looked at him, uncomprehending.

"You asked me," said Trent somehow formally, "to come and talk to your business agent and to you on Sira. I said I'd try, and then I lifted off without doing so. I should apologize."

She looked genuinely bewildered.

"But . . . but that doesn't matter!" she protested. "I—"

"I still have those things to attend to," said Trent. His tone was rueful. "But—"

"But—"

"But then I'll be heading for Loren," he told her. "I'll have to arrange for other ships to come and pick up all the extra people. I . . . I'll be very glad if you'll come on the *Yarrow* when I head for Loren. I can take a few other passengers. You can pick them out, if you like. And . . . ah . . . I won't have business demands on my time between here and Loren."

She stared at him.

"In fact," said Captain Trent, and now he was embarrassed, "in fact I . . . find that I . . . well . . . would like very much to have you as my guest on the *Yarrow*. I like the way you . . . react to emergencies. I'd like to be . . . better acquainted. I've never faced this . . . situation before and I don't know how to say what I mean. I certainly haven't managed to do it so far!"

Marian's expression changed. From seeming bewildered, she looked suddenly and pleasantly understanding.

"But, I think you did!" She smiled at him. "I think you said it beautifully! I'd . . . like to say the same thing as well as you did. Will you pretend that I have?"

Trent looked at once acutely uncomfortable and very much relieved.

"We'll talk it over on the way to Loren."

Then he turned away. Marian smiled after him. And she didn't look in the least puzzled. She smiled very confidently.

On the way to Loren, McHinny insisted that he wanted to show Trent how beautifully his for-the-third-time reconstructed pirate-frustrator worked. He explained that a part he'd used in building the unit for the *Yarrow* had required a certain amount of induction. The idea was that current flowing from the bus-bars to the capacitors had resistance to overcome in the first microseconds of current flow. Therefore the capacitors charged gradually, without overload of the current cables. But the manufactured article in the *Yarrow*'s unit had been defective. With no inductive resistance to control the current going into the gadget, it amounted to a short-circuit. The gadget had blown every time. It couldn't be avoided.

But on the way to the pirate base, said McHinny truculently, the possibility had occurred to him. He'd installed another induction unit in his gadget. And consequently he'd destroyed the one pirate which would otherwise have escaped. Trent opened his mouth to make a correction. The fleeing pirate ship wouldn't have escaped. The mate had orders to blow it with the *Yarrow*'s overdrive if McHinny's gadget didn't work. But then Trent shrugged. It didn't matter.

Now McHinny wanted to show Trent how it worked. Trent took Marian to watch. McHinny swelled with importance and the confidence natural to genius. He threw the charging switch.

And the gadget blew itself to hell and gone.